HOCKEY MANIA
AND
THE MYSTERY
OF
NANCY RUNNING ELK

J. Wayne Frye
Introduction by Jasmine Falling Rain Frye

I0521239

COMMENT TO READERS AND TEACHERS
IN COUNTRIES OTHER THAN CANADA
PLEASE NOTE THAT THIS BOOK IS WRITTEN
IN CANADIAN ENGLISH, SO BE AWARE
OF THE DIFFERENCES
IN THE WAY WORDS ARE SPELLED
IN YOUR OWN COUNTRY

To: *Rachel Fast*, and her father, *Howard Fast*. The two of them made a young man's sojourn in New York City a time when I began to understand the power of words. The nights I spent in Greenwich Village discussing literature opened up a whole new world for me. It just took a few decades for me to realize it. Unlike Howard, I will never write anything as popular or with the eradiation of *Spartacus*, but through his inspirational prose, I have gained immeasurable knowledge in the art of storytelling.

Thanks: To Donald Ferguson whose tales of woe made me want to refine and polish them for the literary world of today.

TABLE OF CONTENTS

Catalogue Number: 20116196109
ISBN: 978-0-9879728-1-1

Produced Under Licence From Fireside Books

**Peninsula Publishing
Victoria, British Columbia**

Cree Lake, Saskatchewan
Home To Hockey Mania & Nancy Running Elk

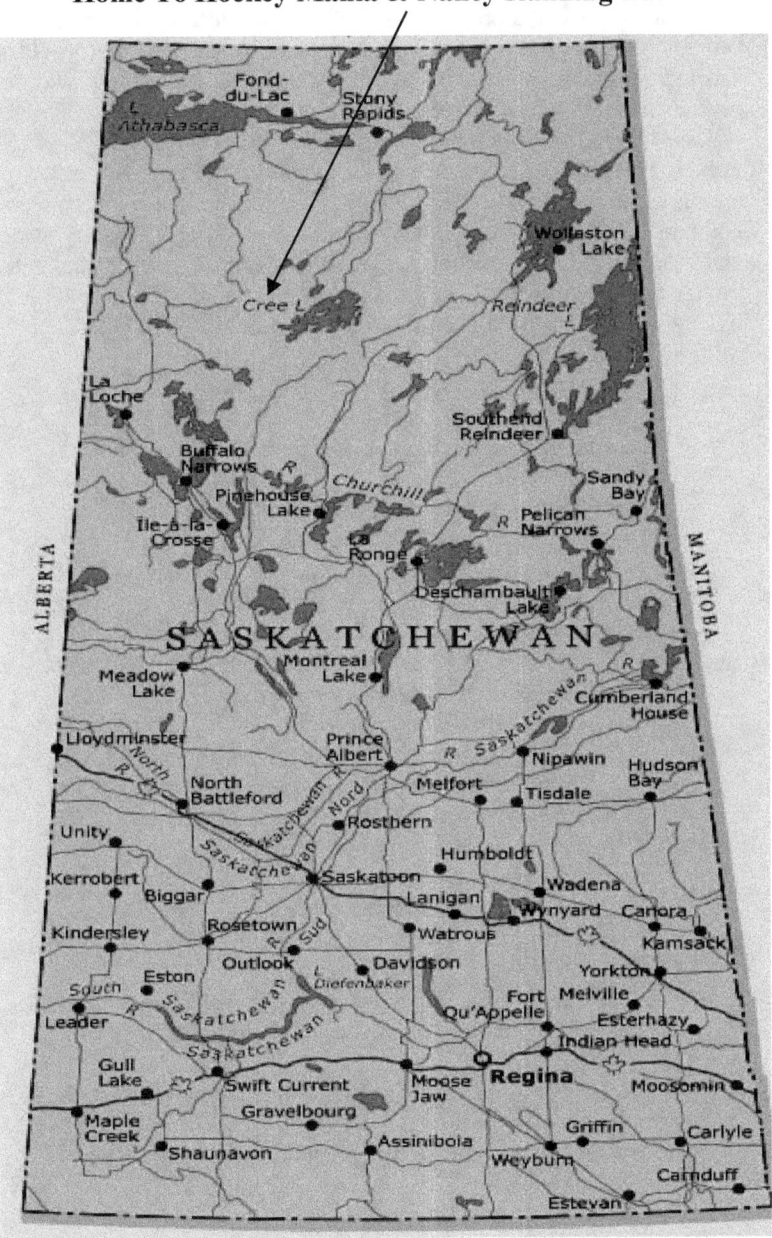

The Author

Wayne Frye's Aaron Adams series has been popular among Canadian mystery lovers since first appearing in 2005. He provides satirical political commentary to many Canadian newspapers, and his books on politics have created a great deal of controversy. He has written marketing/advertising textbooks, been a successful U.S. university hockey coach, professor, university President and served as a marketing consultant to hockey teams and motion picture companies. He has been cited for his work with inner-city gang children in the Los Angeles area and been active in the anti-globalization movement. He became a Canadian citizen in 2003 and lives with his wife in Ladysmith, British Columbia.

Other Books by J. Wayne Frye

Guide to Local Radio and Television Copywriting
Something Evil in the Darkness at Hopkins House
How Hockey Saved a Jew From the Holocaust:
The Rudi Ball Story
The Catastrophic Calamities of a Village Idiot
Fighting for Justice in the Land of Hypocrisy
Guide to Alternative Education (13 Editions)
Cataclysmic Dreams in Black and White
Mastering Marketing Research
Introduction to Advertising
Marketing Plan Work Book
Public Relations Workbook
The Fall From Apocalypse
Advertising Lab Manual
Promotions Workbook
Advertising Design
Armageddon Now
Worth
When Jesus Came to Jersey as the Son of Thunder
The Girl Who Stirred up the Whirlwind

Books by J. Wayne Frye with Jasmine H. Frye

Canadian Angels of Mercy – Nurses in Times of Peril

6

PROLOGUE
JASMINE FALLING RAIN'S INTRODUCTION:
HOCKEY AS A METAPHOR FOR A LIFE
THAT BRINGS OUT THE VERY BEST IN PEOPLE

In all fiction, there is an element of truth. That can certainly be said of this story about Nancy Running Elk and how a hockey coach and two of his players became embroiled in a mystery that would change their lives forever. It is also the story of how a hockey team defied great odds to achieve incredible success both on and off the ice. Ironically, that success actually has nothing to do with winning or losing games.

Readers should be aware that some characters in this story are based upon real-life people, although many characters are composites of individuals, not necessarily one specific person. It is certainly true that fact can often be much stranger than fiction, so on occasion, it is difficult for a writer to separate the two. Facts are details upon which fiction is built. Fiction can assuredly mirror real life. And it is certainly not fiction to state that for the vast majority of Canadians, hockey is an integral part of their lives.

In Canada, hockey is a religion. During the 2010 gold medal game at the Vancouver Olympics, the overtime goal scored by Sidney Crosby that defeated the USA and brought another hockey gold medal to Canada, not only electrified a nation, it proved once again that hockey is a metaphor for life.

The night of that game, there was an old woman suffering from dementia in a Vancouver hospital who had been in a coma for three years. Right before the game went into overtime, as her family sat in her room, watching the game, incredible as it may seem, she came out of the coma, alert and smiling. To everyone's amazement, she asked about the contest, and when told that Canada was battling the USA for the gold medal, she seemed to intently watch the game, while all others in the hospital were scurrying about with the news that she had come out of the coma after three years. Watching Crosby score the winning goal, she said, "we did it." With those words, she closed her eyes and died.

Hockey is a part of the Canadian social structure, and an inextricable part of the country's national identity. Yes, hockey is more than a game to Canadians, and many people in the world cannot understand the connection between the soul of a nation and the game its citizens revere so much. I, as a person born and reared in the USA, had some trouble adjusting to this notion. In 1993, when I met my husband, who was a university hockey coach in Los Angeles, and first became exposed to a game that I sometimes think he may love more than me, it did not dawn on me how important it would also become in my own life.

How often, when he will occasionally watch a game on the computer (we have no television), have I heard the refrain "these guys are over-paid prima-donnas who play for money, not for love of the game. You want to see real hockey, go to the adult leagues, go to the junior games, go watch the kids play. That is the soul of the game."

He exhibits general frustration with those who cannot see the underlying reason for being on the ice is not just to play a game, but to engage in a titanic struggle that represents the underlying truth of what is possible for those willing to sacrifice together in order to reach a common goal. He truly sees the hockey rink as an arena where the last of the gladiators in a world ruled by a corporate theocracy can do battle free of the artificial barriers placed by a world where greed rules supreme.

Population-wise, Canada is a relatively small country. It is a nation with a much more populated and powerful southern neighbour that often overshadows it. Perhaps this helps Canadians to understand that life, in the end, is just one long sudden-death overtime that you do not always win. Winning all the time gives you a false sense of life and fosters a feeling of entitlement like many of the world's royals exhibit, as they see themselves chosen by God, when, in fact, they are nothing more than the beneficiaries of a privileged birth. Life (as most Canadians understand it) is a series of tiny overtime losses, to be managed quietly, without much fuss. Canadians hopes are private and small. The very idea of victory is something reserved for story books. As a nation, Canada can come to terms with the fact that it does not always win. Consequently, its citizens have internalized the absurdity of measuring life as a win-loss record, conducting themselves from day to day outside the victor/vanquished binary, content that most problems can be diminished to the size of a hockey rink and settled on a frozen surface of honour. For that reason, its citizens see fit to offer reasons for contentment. Sure, this mindset means fewer winners at the top, but it also means fewer losers at the bottom of society.

Despite this attitude, there are still gaps in any society where worth is too often judged by economic or social status. Despite great strides for social justice in Canada, years of abuse, neglect and prejudice perpetrated against Aboriginals cannot be wiped out with the mere stroke of a pen. There are still pockets of injustice that Canadians must be eternally vigilant against, as we continue in the fight for a truly just and equal society.

From the very beginning, ice hockey was more than a mere game. It was first observed by Europeans being played by Micmac Indians in Nova Scotia in the late 1600's. It was called ricket by the Natives. The game was played utilizing a frozen road apple as the first puck. The game is played today much the same as it was then, only with the addition of some modern equipment.

As a proud member of the First Nations and the wife of a former hockey coach, I take great pride in having helped formulate, develop and refine the ideas for this story that you are about to read. Although not completely factual, it is based on the experiences of my husband and I over a two year period that helped the two of us better appreciate all the possibilities offered by a life unencumbered with the conventionalities under which the vast majority of humanity labours. It further helps us all understand how a simple game can bring out the very best in people.

Jasmine Falling Rain Frye

Reference for life quote: Jonny Diamond. October 10, 2011.

CHAPTER 1
WONDERING JUST WHAT MONTE MEANT

Monte Running Bear looked at the big thermometer hanging precariously above the door of the downtown's only remaining un-deserted building. Housing the grocery store, post office and a small coffee shop, it was the hub of activity in the small village of Cree Lake. It was getting cold, and in Northern Saskatchewan that meant only one thing. The first snowstorm wasn't far off and before long the ponds would be frozen, and Monte and the rest of the boys could start playing shinny hockey. Eventually Cree Lake itself would be frozen, then they could scrape the snow to the sides, smooth it out and put up the plywood boards that gave this isolated village of 1205 people a hockey rink. The bigger villages, towns and cities had indoor rinks, but this was just a small Reserve, so while the boys in the big city got to play indoors, the Cree boys had to play hockey the old-fashioned way – outdoors in the cold, snow and fierce winds that blew in off the plains. Hey, there weren't even any roads into Cree Lake. They did have an airport, so food and medical supplies could be brought in during the winter. Most months of the year, there was an accessible old service road that connected the village to Missinipe, 125 kilometres (78 miles) to the south, where the nearest paved road into civilization was available. Yet, the isolation never bothered Monte until the winter months, when visiting other villages to play hockey was often difficult because of the weather.

Turning to his friend Ted, Monte said, "feels like it will be hockey time soon. I would guess the ponds should freeze over tonight. I bet our friend Tom Miller's knees are already getting sore. His knees can always tell when winter is about to arrive."

11

Ted Ironchest had been Monte's best friend since they were old enough to play floor hockey together as three year olds in their mother's kitchens. Whereas Monte was a somewhat muscular 17 year old, Ted was only slightly taller than a husky dog standing on its hind legs and so slight in build that it appeared a mild breeze might tip him over. Yet, when Ted laced up his skates, he towered over every other player in terms of drive, desire and determination. He didn't have the athletic ability Monte had, but he made up for his lack of talent with heart. You could see the anticipation in his eyes when he said, "we want to test ourselves before we go up against Stony Narrows. It may always be our first game, but if we don't win it, we seem to have a crisis of confidence every year. If the ponds freeze over, I am sure the elders will call for a try-out game this Saturday. The whole band is tired of having a losing record every year. I even heard old Riddick say to another elder that they shouldn't even put up stands this year, because people are getting tired of always watching us lose."

The two boys, who had just left the home of a schoolmate named Hatto Stalking Moon, were not only the two best hockey players in the village, they were also well-known for being difficult to coach, as were most of the other players. In fact, it was often difficult to find a coach for the town's midget team, because of its reputation for being undisciplined.

Yet, of all the team's players, Monte was the coolest and calmest, while Ted was constantly showing visible signs of great excitement. Monte could control his temper on the ice under intense provocation, but poor old Ted seemed to often go berserk at the least physical affront that might be presented by an opposing player.

12

It was already the 18th of September, and thus far the opportunities for skating that had come to the potential players was non-existent. Meanwhile, in the larger villages and towns, indoor rinks were giving other players a chance to skate while the Cree Lake players waited for cold weather. Unfortunately, with global warming, each year the freezing of the ponds and lake seemed to come later and later. Both boys took a look back at the thermometer, and smiled at each other when they noticed it had just dipped below freezing and it was only noon.

Cree Lake had two keen rivals in Northern Saskatchewan, Stony Narrows and Sandy Lake. The teams from Saskatoon and Regina usually won the Provincial Championship, but the Northern area always came down to two teams, either Stony Narrows or Sandy Lake. Cree Lake had given them a few tough contests over the years, but they had not won a game from either team in almost ten years. The townspeople had pretty much lost interest in hockey, especially the last three years when the new crop of players seemed to just be un-coachable. Seven coaches in three years had tried their hand at getting them under control, but only one coach was able to last through a complete season, and he was so frustrated that he wound up in a psychiatric ward in New Battleford after the season was over.

Yet, this year, the Tribal Council had decided to erect stands on one side of the lake to accommodate up to 200 people for the games. After all, what else did people in Cree Lake have to do on a Friday or Saturday nights? There was no cable TV in town, and even satellite TV was prone to interference from the Northern Lights. No one had even come forward to coach this year, but still it seemed that the stage was being set for something unique.

Over the next week, winter arrived in full force and the ponds, the downtown parking lot and the lake had been groomed and prepped for skating. Yet, there had been no midget team tryouts announced, while all the other divisions already had teams. Was the village just going o give up on fielding a midget team this year? Hey, maybe they couldn't find anyone willing to coach a bunch of rogues who had chased off every coach that dared make an attempt to control the uncontrollable.

At school, Monte was having trouble with the designated harlot, female bully and general pariah, Nancy Running Elk. Ever since the summer, they had been at odds over a variety of issues.

Apparently, something was bothering Ted, judging from the way in which he several times looked queerly at Monte with troubled eyes that seemed to be pleading for an explanation of what was going on since Monte had been spending so little time with him the past week. Finally, as if determined to speak up, he said, half apologetically. "Monte, excuse me if I'm butting in where I have no business, but when I saw you talking so long with that nasty girl, Nancy Running Elk, today, I was concerned. Was she threatening you with violence again? After that verbal fight the two of you had this summer, I assumed you two would no longer be talking at all."

Monte chuckled, as though the recollection might not be wholly displeasing. "Oh! no, you're way off in your guess, Ted," he replied immediately. "Fact is, instead of threats, Nancy was asking a favour of me."

"You got to be kidding!" interjected Ted. "Well, now you've got my interest piqued."

Monte replied, "It seems that for a long time she's been admiring those old hockey skates of mine. In fact, she asked me to sell them to her since she heard I had bought new skates."

"Well," commented Ted, "we all know that Nancy is a great skater, but she has never showed any interest in hockey. I would think she is a bit old to start playing now. Besides, there are no girl's teams and her on-ice temperament would probably be worse than mine, if her off-ice temperament is any indication."

"You're painting Nancy pretty true to life, Ted," agreed Monte; "though I'm sorry it's so, I've got a hunch that girl, might make a pretty good player. I have seen her play pick-up with some of the older men in the band with those old skates she bought from the thrift store. She ain't half bad. In fact, she is a remarkable playmaker."

"Are you going to sell the skates?"

"No, I told her I didn't care to sell them," Monte replied. "I was tempted to agree, but she looked at me so harshly, like she was still carrying a grudge over the argument we had in the summer, that I just said I wasn't interested."

"Perhaps," said Ted a bit wistfully, "you might bequeath me your old skates. Mine are shot."

Monte, with a smile creasing his lips, said, "I'll remember you in my will."

Ted, reflecting on how much he detested Nancy, said, "you know, I don't really think you should even consider giving that dork the time of the day. She is the biggest jerk in this entire village, and if people see you talking to her, they will begin to think you are a jerk, too. Excuse me, what am I saying, everybody in town already thinks you and I are both jerks, anyway. In fact, they think our whole team is a bunch of jerks. Still, I say keep away from her."

Monte, in a serious tone replied, "Speak for yourself. I've got an inkling to tell you something that's been on my mind lately."

Ted, his eyes beaming with a tint of indignation, said nothing, but he was wondering just what Monte meant.

CHAPTER 2
THE SKATES HAD DISAPPEARED

Building up his courage, Ted became more indignant as he thought about why his friend apparently was holding something back. Finally, he instinctively blurted out, "don't play games with me, there is something amiss. What is it?"

"Oh! just a little speculation I've been indulging in. Wondering if she might be just that extra bit of talent we need to make the team more formidable."

Ted, almost laughing out-loud, said, "a girl on our team? You can't be serious. None of the guys would tolerate it. Anyway, she is a bigger juvenile delinquent than we are. To top it off, she has the morals of an alley cat. She had a kid when she was 14. She may be a little pretty on the outside, but inside she is as ugly as they come."

Monte, in a stern and assured manner, seemed taken aback by his friend's disdain for Nancy. "I think otherwise. You get to know her, and she is a pretty nice person. She puts up a tough front, because she has to in order to survive in this place where people are too quick to point the finger of condemnation."

Warming a bit to what his friend was saying, Ted became a bit more receptive. "I suppose its possible that people can be misjudged. After all, we aren't as bad as people make us out to be. We just kind of live up to what we think is expected of us. People give us a bad reputation with their gossip, so we just sort of figure we might as well live up to it. One time I would like to have a coach or a teacher who could forget our reputation and give us a fresh start."

Monte, surprised that his friend was engaging in a philosophical discussion, said, "too many people around here think we are just a bunch of worthless malcontents. Maybe we are malcontents, because nobody will give us a chance. They are even worse when dealing with Nancy. Maybe that is why she is so combative with people. She is just giving back what she gets. I know how she feels. We are taught about honour and justice, but when do we see any? The government gives all of us medical care. They give us a place to live. They pay for our education. Yet, we had our way of life destroyed by the same government that has made us wards of the state. They think we are supposed to forget the past. How can we forget the past? Because of the way our parents, grandparents and great grandparents were treated – often being stolen from their loved ones and carted off to residential schools to be indoctrinated in the white man's religion and the white man's morals – we are lost in a world we didn't create and don't understand."

Ted, surprised at his friend's wisdom and eloquent expression of frustration stared in bewilderment, but did manage to utter a few equally eloquent words of his own. "Yeah, you got it right buddy. I am not looking for excuses, but I am tired of being told how useless I am, because I don't want the same things others do. Why do we need expensive sneakers, fancy cars, big screen TV's and all the other things we are told make life worth living. Why can't we be happy just being ourselves, rather than being what others tell us we have to be? Most grown-ups in this town are slaves, and they don't even realize it. They let others tell them what to do and what to believe,

18

and they want us to be the same way. Even the teachers don't want us to question authority. We are just supposed to do what we are told without ever asking why."

Both boys were surprised at themselves, as they continued their exploration of who they were. Monte, the most irreverent of the two could not resist continuing on the topic. "You know, I would like to meet just one person in this town who could look at us without disdain. I know we have done things that we shouldn't, but isn't there a single person who can realize that no matter how low a person sinks, they should be given a chance to climb up out of despair?"

Then, they both laughed out loud, shook their heads and realized that they were just being foolish. Nothing would ever change in Cree Lake. Ted became less philosophical and more practical when he said, "That just doesn't work in real life and we know it. Prisons are full of people like us who don't get with the programme. And poor old Nancy Running Elk is on Constable McMillan's hit list. He is determined to get that girl locked up."

Monte replied, "well, as much as I hate to side with Constable McMillan, you have to admit that Nancy has certainly made life miserable for the entire police force around here. She started brush fires just to watch the volunteer fire-fighters run around in a frenzy. Even stood there and laughed when they were falling all over each other trying to put out the fire. Then she got a garden hose and put it out while the fire-fighters were still trying to unwind their own hose. She is always stealing apples from the Johnson's farm, but justifies it by saying they had already fallen on the ground. And what about the time she let a skunk lose in the school auditorium, because she felt we all needed a vacation from school. It took two days for a fumigator to come up from New Battleford to get rid of the smell. Oh yeah, what about the time she hung up pictures of Karl Marx all along the parade route when that

Conservative Party official was in town? Is it any wonder that Constable McMillan has it in for her? She is not exactly a model citizen."

Unable to contain his glee over recalling some of Nancy's more outlandish pranks, Ted was almost laughing when he offered a sage observation. "I've an idea that once in awhile some of the more respected people in town may have committed certain acts and felt pretty safe in doing them, because every citizen would believe Nancy was the culprit."

Sighing, the two walked away together and no more was said on that subject, though afterwards Ted had it brought to his attention again, and in a peculiar way at that.

The two boys separated a little further on, each heading homeward. On the following morning it was found that their predictions concerning the weather had been amply verified. The mercury had dropped down in the tube of the thermometer, and every youngster had a happy look on his or her face at school, as though the prospect for skating brought almost universal satisfaction. Hockey season was about to start in the little hamlet of Cree Lake.

Ted, with several others, had gone out to Chief Thundercloud pond to try the newly frozen ice. Monte wanted to accompany them, but he had promised his mother to spend a couple of hours that afternoon helping around the house. And once his word was given, Monte never broke it, no matter how alluring the prospect of playing hockey might be. Also, he knew that he had often caused his mother much consternation, and even though it seemed impossible for him to avoid trouble, he was always respectful of her.

It was about 3 o'clock in the afternoon. Monte sat in his den amidst his prized possessions – which consisted of all the hockey trophies and paraphernalia he had accumulated over the years. Of course, hanging over the fireplace was his most prized possession, a huge framed poster of a toothless Bobby Clarke in 1975 holding up the Stanley Cup. He had heard many tales of Clarke over the years from a former Band Chief who had lived in Flin Flon, Manitoba when Clarke played for the Flin Flon Bombers. In fact, Monte had always patterned his style of play after Clarke. Like Clarke, Monte never backed down on the ice, and no one could ever question his dedication to hard work and consistency. Yet, he, like the rest of the team, had a rebellious streak in him that just seemed to frustrate coach after coach.

He was working on his lessons to get them out of the way, as there was a dance scheduled for that evening, which he meant to attend; and he would be too tired if he skated all day. Anyway, he had heard Nancy tell another girl that she was going to the dance, and Monte felt that he really wanted to see her for a reason he couldn't really fathom. It couldn't be that he was actually interested in her romantically. After all, Monte was known at school as "the stud of Cree Lake," so he could get any girl he wanted, and he certainly didn't want Nancy. Anyway, no boy ever really had anything to do with Nancy. She had treated boys with disdain ever since she was 14 and got pregnant by some unknown boy from who knows where. Since then, she had lived in disgrace, and was shunned by most of her fellow students and the moral upper-crust citizens who ran the village.

Several times he glanced over to where his carefully polished and well-sharpened skates, strapped together, lay on a side table. Each look caused him to shrug his shoulders a bit. He could easily imagine he heard the delightful clang of steel runners cutting into that smooth sheet of new ice out at the pond; and the figures of the happy skaters would pass before his eyes. Yes, probably Sue Charlie would be there, too, with her friends, Ivy Joe and Peggy Bill. They were affectionately called Charlie, Joe and Bill by their friends. Their last names were just another example of the cruelty perpetrated on the Aboriginals by their white overlords. When their parents had been taken away to residential schools, their native last names were changed, and generally the names taken were actually the favourite first names of the white Christians who locked them up to force them to become more civilized.

Then, Monte heaved a little sigh, and applied himself harder than ever to his task. When he had an unpleasant thing to do, he never allowed temptation to swerve him. And, after all, it was pretty snug and comfortable there in his den. Yet, in the back of his mind was a flicker, a vision that seemed locked into everything he had been doing lately. He could see Nancy's face with those thick, soft lips and those mischievous eyes twinkling beneath her thick, dark eye brows that arced ever so slightly. What was wrong with him? She was short, slightly overweight and her personality – well, that was as volatile as a badger cornered in a pit. Just as he was about to tell himself that he had to get her off his mind, he heard his mother speaking to someone who must have come to the front door.

"Go up to the top of the stairs, and turn to the right. You will find him in the den, I believe. Monte, are you there? There's a visitor to see you."

Supposing, of course, that it must be one of his close friends, who for some reason had not gone off skating, and wished to see him about some matter of importance, Monte, after answering his mother, had continued his work.

He heard the door open, and close softly. Then someone gave a gruff cough in an attempt to get him to look up. Monte looked around and received quite a surprise. Standing before him in a buckskin dress was none other than Nancy Running Elk. Her long, shiny coal black hair had two locks gracefully hanging on the right side in curls. Around her head was a multi-coloured band. Her gaze was intense and her eye lids were not blinking at all. Monte thought to himself that if she had some war paint on, he might be in trouble.

"Oh, hello, Nancy!" he commenced to say, a little restrained in his welcome; for, of course, he knew why she was there. She wanted his skates.

He pushed a chair forward, determined not to be uncivil at any rate. Of course, he did not realize the very act of pushing her a chair was, in itself, disrespectful. Perhaps that is why Nancy did not sit. Rather she stood there with a stern look on her face.

The outlook was far from promising. Indeed, he could not remember ever seeing Nancy look more antagonistic than just then, even though he tried to appear friendly.

Rather curtly, Monte said, "You wanted to see me about something, Nancy?"

Nancy eased into the chair. Her furtive gaze went around the room as if it aroused her curiosity, for this was really the first occasion she had ever been in Monte's house. As she scanned the room, her eyes alighted on the coveted skates. Nancy's face took on an expressive grin. Then she turned toward Monte, to say, almost whiningly, "Sure thing, Monte. I thought maybe I'd coax you to let me have the skates, if I told you I'd managed to get twenty dollars by selling some rabbits to the Conklin's. Here's a twenty; take it, and give me the skates, won't you?"

Her manner was intended to be ingratiating, but evidently Nancy was so accustomed to bullying everyone with whom she came in contact that it was next to impossible for her to change her abusive demeanour. Monte felt less inclined than ever to accommodate her. Under other and more favourable conditions he might have been tempted to promise Nancy the skates for nothing. Still, in the back of his mind was that image of Nancy that would not go away. What was wrong with him? He was not going to let this overwhelm him. He was not going to be enamoured with Nancy, no way. He decided to be belligerent.

"I have told you no already, Nancy."

"But there's nothing to hinder you selling them. Are you just refusing because of a grudge against me. Come on

Monte," Nancy said in a more demure and less combative way.

Still Monte did not like the feelings that were manifesting themselves in his mind. He did not want to be romantically interested in Nancy, and he would prove it to himself by refusing to sell her the skates. He fought his feelings with curtness toward Nancy. "I told you that I am not interested in selling them to you."

Nancy was getting a bit perturbed. "That's it. I know the real reason. The key is the word me. Because it is me, you aren't interested. I notice the way you look at me, especially when you think I don't see you looking. You like me, but you don't want to admit it. Well, guess what? I not only don't like you, I don't even want you to like me. It is disgusting to think of you liking me, because you just think I am easy. Well, ask any boy in town. I am not easy. They all know it, because they have all tired. You are an arrogant egotist who thinks all the girls are gaga over you. Well, this one isn't."

Monte, sitting behind a desk, placed his hands on it and smiled in defiance of Nancy's tirade. Meanwhile, Nancy had shuffled away, as though meaning to sneakily leave the room. When Monte looked up, she had managed to get half-way through the door, and turned to say with a sneer, "I am not going to forget this Monte, believe me. I thought I'd give you a chance to smooth over the rough places between us; but you keep telling yourself that you don't want anything to do with a person who has the reputation I do. Of course, secretly you do want to have something to do with me. That is your problem. Alright, keep your old skates then, and you know what you can do with them."

In spite of her attitude, as she hurried out the door and scurried down the stairs, Monte sat still at the desk, contemplating what had just occurred. She had ridiculed and belittled him, but there they were again – those visions of her in the back of his mind. He glanced over to his right where the skates had been and made a startling discovery. The skates had disappeared!

CHAPTER 3
MISCHEVIOUS TWINKLE IN NANCY'S EYES

Jumping to his feet, Monte ran to the table by the window and just stood there, staring down at where his skates should have been. Looking to the left, under a coaster, he saw a 20 dollar bill. She paid for his skates.

Thinking hard as he stared at the 20 dollar bill, he concluded that she had not exactly stolen the skates. At least that was the way she probably saw it. She lifted the skates, but by leaving the 20 dollars, she was actually paying for them.

Monte at first felt indignant. He gave the money an angry look, as though scorning it. He thought to himself that it didn't matter. She was contemptible to think she had the right to walk out with the skates when he wasn't willing to sell.

Aroused by the sense of injustice, and a desire to turn the tables on the slippery Nancy, he stepped forward to snatch up his cap, with the full intention of hurrying out to see if he could overtake the thief; and, if not, continuing on until he came to the office of the constable. Then he stopped short with a gasp. He had suddenly remembered something. There was that vision of Nancy in the back of his mind again.

He dropped back into his seat, with the money gripped in his hand. He stared intensely at it. In his imagination he could see Nancy, working hard to earn that money, because her grandmother, with whom she lived, certainly wouldn't have given it to her. She must have done considerable work to earn that money. She wanted that pair of skates really bad. For years he had seen her out there on the pond practicing by herself in an old pair of skates that looked like they were left over from the 1940's.

Yes, Nancy must have wanted his old skates worse than she ever wanted anything in all her life. And when he refused to sell them, she just thought she would do the trading by herself. It was an incredibly queer way of doing business, and one the law would obviously not recognize; but, after all, it was Monte who was considering suggesting that she suit up for the team. With her tenacity and innate ability, she would be an asset to a team that desperately needed a gifted playmaker. He mused over it for several minutes. Then the sound of voices outside caught his attention. One seemed to be gruff and official, another a bit high-pitched and desperate sounding.

Monte jumped up and stepped gingerly to the window. He could see down to the end of the street where three people were desperately hurrying toward his house. One of these he recognized as Ted, who must have returned from the pond as he was carrying his skates and hockey stick. Another was the rotund, but muscular, Constable McMillan, and the party whom he was gripping by the arm—yes, it was none other than the thief, Nancy Running Elk.

He realized that, undoubtedly, by some strange freak of fortune, Ted must have seen Nancy gloating over her new prized possession; and recognizing the skates, he had beckoned to the constable, who happened to be near by, that Nancy should be nabbed before she could get away with the theft.

Monte had to decide quickly as to what he should do, for they were coming in through the front gate. Once again in the back of his mind fluttered images of Nancy. He thought to himself – brain, stop it.

Ted knew how to get in by the side door that opened on the back stairs; so he did not waste any time in ringing the bell. Now, Monte could hear heavy footsteps. They were coming, and the great test was about to be made.

The door opened to admit, first of all, Ted, his face filled with burning indignation, and his eyes sparkling with excitement. Close on his heels, the others also pushed into the room. Constable McMillan looked triumphant and grim. Nancy fairly writhed in the iron grip of the burly officer, and her face had assumed a red colour as her blood was apparently pumping furiously from fear and excitement. With pleading eyes she looked directly at Monte.

Letting go of her, Constable McMillan snarled, "stand still you little thief. Move and I will taser you."

Now it was the excited Ted's turn to speak. "Monte, this little miscreant has robbed you.. I saw her prancing down the street swinging your skates in her right hand. I would know your skates anywhere. Anyway, they have your initials carved on the blades. I summoned the constable to apprehend her, because he was at the Morgan's house. and I told him about it. He made Nancy come back here to face you and confess to the theft."

Nancy growled furiously, "I didn't steal anything. You all just want me locked up. I am the favourite punching bag for the whole town."

McMillan simply said, "shut up, thief."

The stiff-backed McMillan, with his chest defiantly puffed out, held up the skates. "Ted tells me that these are yours. He even showed me where your initials were carved. Look at them closely before I lug this thief off to jail. She's been in jail before, and she needs to be there again for the safety of the community."

At that outburst, Nancy's shoulders dropped and you could see her whole demeanour seemingly collapse in fright. You could see the fear in her eyes.

Monte reached out and calmly looked the skates over. Nancy was intently watching his every move. She thought that it was all over. Juvenile detention loomed up dreadfully in her mind, darker than she had ever before imagined it. The thought of being away from her child made her shiver. Yet, what could she do? Her fate was in Monte's hands.

"Yes, I recognize these skates." Monte told the waiting officer.

"And do they belong to you?" Continued the officer, with a stern look at the cringing culprit near by, who weakly leaned on the table where the skates had been.

"They were my property until just a few minutes ago. Then I had a very generous offer from Nancy to buy them. At first I was averse to letting her purchase them, as they have sentimental value, but I changed my mind. She has great persuasive powers, so great that it is difficult to say no to her. So, I finally agreed that she should have them."

Monte was looking directly at Nancy. "These skates belong Nancy," he said, as he reached down and picked up the 20 dollar bill, waving it in front of the constable.

The constable got a grim look on his face and sighed in a somewhat juvenile manner as he turned to Nancy. Just as he did, Monte said, "folks are going to be amazed at the team we field this year, because Nancy is going to be the first girl to play for the Midgets. You'll have to come out to some games and cheer for us Constable McMillan."

McMillan didn't say a word in response. He just walked out the door, disappointed that he would not be able to lock-up Nancy.

Meanwhile, Nancy stealthily exited almost unnoticed by the two boys. Monte told Ted the whole story, but swore him to secrecy.

The sceptical Ted was having none of it. "I wish you success in your experiment in psychology, Monte, but I don't believe for a minute the leopard is going to change its spots, or that Nancy, the worst girl in town, is worthy of your compassion."

That night Monte went to the dance. While there, as usual, he had girls begging for his attention, but he was constantly ignoring them and glancing out of the corner of his eyes, looking over near the back door of the dance hall, where Nancy stood holding her child, talking with her grandmother and two tribal elders.

Upon returning home, he crept into bed and lay there looking out of the window where a bright star hung above the horizon. It seemed to twinkle incessantly. It reminded him of something. It was like that mischievous twinkle in Nancy's eyes.

CHAPTER 4
THE CREE LAKE BADGERS WERE A TEAM

Wayne Wellman's wife, Janice, was a kind soul who had always dreamed of working with what she called "her people." Although not a Cree, she was Aboriginal, and as the new Nurse Practitioner in town, she was just becoming adjusted to a small community after living in a large urban area. She was already becoming known as a caring person, who was always concerned with the welfare of her patients. Her much older husband, had cheerfully followed her to Cree Lake, since, as a writer, he could live almost anywhere. However, unbeknownst to people in town, Wayne had also been a successful university hockey coach. And therein lies the next thread in the story of how hockey mania gripped this remote little village.

The first day of tryouts for the town's midget team, only 18 players showed up, as it appeared the team would be made up of exactly the same rogues as the previous year's squad. No one had even offered to coach at this point, because last year's team literally had two coaches quit by throwing up their arms and walking off the bench during games in disgust over the unruliness of the players. The third and final coach, lasted the last 7 games of the season, but not only refused to never coach them again, he threatened to file a law suit against the town for luring him in to coach under false pretences by not telling him how much trouble the players were.

Monte was particularly bewildered, because Nancy was conspicuously absent. It made him wonder why he had gone to so much trouble to save her from the long arm of the law.

Wayne Wellman stood stoically by and watched a couple of men try and conduct a practice, but they were obviously not able to control the unruly group of players. As he turned to walk-away, a man came up to him and said, "aren't you Wayne Wellman? "

"Yes, do I know you," replied Wayne.

"Not really, but I know you. I was at a university that used to play the team you coached on occasion. You kicked our butts every time. What are you doing up here?"

"My wife is the new Nurse Practitioner for the town."

Extending his hand, the tall, thin man of perhaps 40 said, "I am Lance Thundercloud. I guess you notice that we could use a coach. Frankly, these kids have pretty much proven that they are un-coachable. They have gone through 7 coaches in the three years they have played together. No one is interested in dealing with them, so we may not even field a midget team this year."

Wayne, his interest piqued, said, "so, why are they so much trouble?"

"Just a group who have been trouble since they were young kids. They actually have some talent, but absolutely no discipline. Any kind of authority is subject to suspicion by them. They are all rogues, I'm afraid."

Wayne, smiling, replied. "hey, I have always been a rogue myself. I belief questioning authority is fundamental to an inquisitive mind. If a few more people had questioned authority in Germany, there would have been no Holocaust. If a few more people had questioned authority in the USA, there would have been no torture in Guantanamo, Iraq or Afghanistan."

Thundercloud stood in silence for what seemed like an eternity, before he came out with a question that began a saga that would bring incredible excitement to the little remote corner of the world called Cree Lake. "So, you want to coach these rogues?"

Rubbing his face with his right hand as in deep thought, Wayne enthusiastically replied, "sure, what else do I have to do?"

Thus began the saga of the Cree Lake Badgers, and a season that would go down in the annals of Saskatchewan hockey history. The Band Council approved Wellman as coach that night, and the following day, the players would be in for a big surprise.

That afternoon the same 18 players showed up for practice, and Wellman introduced himself. Not making any note of his hockey history, the players were not particularly impressed with his hockey knowledge, but they did go through their drills with a bit more intensity than usual, as they seemed pleased that someone was willing to tackle the daunting task of coaching the un-coachable. After practice, as the players sat on the benches by the pond, removing their equipment, Wellman sat down and talked with each one individually, asking about mundane things that had nothing to do with hockey. Many actually thought that he was a bit too inquisitive about their school work and their home life. What was this guy, a coach or a social worker? Little did the players know this was just the beginning of what was a grand plan for establishing a camaraderie that would lead to a team that would stand by one another and their coach through an incredible season that would be like no other they had ever experienced.

As Monte and Ted grabbed their equipment bags and started to leave, Wellman quickly stepped in front of them and made a stop motion with both of his hands in front of his chest. "Gentlemen, we wait for the coach to dismiss the team from the locker room. I have a few things to say before you can leave."

Not wanting to create problems the first day of practice with the new coach, Ted and Monte willingly sat back down. It was then that Wellman said what would stick with each player throughout the season. They were simple words, but came from the heart. "Gentlemen, I have been offered some very unflattering tales about you and this team. I have even been offered dossiers on each one of you. Apparently, you all have many detractors who think that you are rogues of the worst kind. I refused to listen to any gossip, and I would not entertain the thought of looking at your individual files that were compiled by a variety of people. I respect the fact that you are all intelligent individuals who are destined for greatness on the ice. I saw that possibility in the way you performed in practice today. But, I also think you can be destined for greatness in your personal life off the ice. Whatever happened in the past is just that – it is the past. From this day on, we move forward together as a team. See you here tomorrow at 4:00 for practice, and remember that I go by Vince Lombardi time. If practice is at 4:00 and you don't show up at 3:30, you are late. For those of you who don't know who Vince Lombardi was, look it up. See you tomorrow."

The players looked at one another quizzically. Was Wellman telling the truth? Was he wiping the slate clean?

As Wellman turned and started to walk away, Monte ran up to him and said, "hey coach, we are short two players. Want to do a little recruiting?"

Wellman, replied, "I am all ears. You have someone special in mind?"

"There's a girl named Nancy Running Elk who is a great skater and terrific playmaker. The problem is getting her to suit up. Of course, if you got a problem with a girl playing on a boy's team at this level, I understand."

"Gender isn't important, Monte. Even talent is not always important, because lack of talent can often be overcome with desire and determination. I'll look her up and invite her to practice."

Wellman immediately left practice, went to the Tribal Elders' Office and asked where to locate Nancy Running Elk. As he approached her house on the outskirts of town, he noticed two girls skating and passing the puck on a nearby pond. Ambling over and watching for a few minutes, he was mesmerized by the smooth, fluid skating and the pinpoint passing. The girls looked his way, and he motioned for them to come over. They skated to him, stopping abruptly and sprayed ice on him when they dug their skates deep into the ice.

Wellman laughed and said, "you girls are pretty fluid skaters. I am Wayne Wellman, the new midget coach. You know Nancy Running Elk by any chance? I'm trying to recruit her for the team."

The taller of the two replied, "yeah, I know her, I'm her friend, Myrna St. John, and belief me, she is not the kind of person you want on your team. She is sassy, selfish with the puck and can't control her temper. She would spend most of her time in the penalty box. Besides, the boys would not like a girl on their team."

"That's interesting, a boy named Monte Running Bear is the one who recommended her."

The smaller girl, seemingly in deep thought, in a barely audible voice said, "Monte."

"Yeah, you know him?"

Smiling broadly with eyes that had a mischievous twinkle, she could not hold her delight back at hearing Monte was the one who recommended Nancy. "I know him. I am Nancy Running Elk."

Thus, that day Wellman not only recruited Nancy, he got another exceptional player named Myrna St. John in the bargain. The rest is history.

The rag-tag pack of malcontents practiced three hours every day, and the two girls were such great players, who asked no quarter and gave no quarter, that the team seemed to coalesce around the pair. In fact, right before the opening game of the season, the team voted Nancy captain and selected Monte and Myrna as alternates.

Word had gotten around that the troubled team was showing signs of improvement, and just maybe the team could actually be a worthy representative of Cree Lake. The first game was at home against arch-rival Stony

Narrows. They came in by plane for the two games that would be played Friday night and Saturday afternoon. There was a large crowd present to watch the match that night. In fact all 200 seats were filled and people started going to the town hall and bringing out folding seats to put along the shore line. Not only were school pupils interested, but many of the town folks seemed to find it convenient to stroll around town and somehow wind up at the game. In fact, Nancy's grandmother was sitting in the front row, proudly holding Nancy's 2 year old daughter and pointing enthusiastically, telling her, "That's Mama there. Wave at her."

Now that the high board-fence surrounded the rink, the carefully planned game seemed to elicit a feeling of pride in those who attended.

The two goals in the centre of the extreme ends were stationary, the posts having been rooted to the ice in some ingenious fashion, with the nets between. The referee delayed the game, because only bendable rubber was permitted for posts, and it took about 30 minutes to locate the rubber posts, remove the stationary ones and install the regulation posts.

Since it was the first game, each player was introduced. The last two, Nancy Running Elk and Myrna St. John, skated to centre ice and were met with a thundering ovation. This was a first, two girls on a boys midget team.

The referee for the game was Leonard Running Bear, who had never looked on Cree Lake with favour in any games he had refereed. In fact, he seemed to have a great deal of animosity for what he saw as a team made up of ill-tempered malcontents. When he skated over to the

Cree Lake bench, he sternly told the team before the game started that he meant to be severe in inflicting punishment and penalties. Since he had not skated over to the visiting team's bench, Wellman looked at him and said, "I assume you are gong to provide the same admonition to the Stony Narrows team. My team knows how to play the game fairly, but they will play with intensity."

The team looked at their coach admiringly for standing up for them. This guy had their back, and would not tolerate anyone treating them unfairly.

The game began, and was soon in full progress, with the players furiously surging from one end of the rink to the other. Wellman's team left the ice littered with bodies as their furious but legal checking seemed to catch the Stony Narrows team off-guard. Yet, penalty after penalty was assessed against Cree Lake by a referee who seemed to look at even a legal check as an affront to his pre-game admonition to Cree Lake. Before more than half of the first twenty-minute period had been exhausted, the score was 5-0 in favour of Stony Narrows.

Then the tactics of Cree Lake underwent a change. The coach, for the first time, put a line out made up of Monte, Nancy and Myrna. In a fashion truly miraculous, Nancy managed to gain possession of the rubber on the face-off, and the way in which she sent it flying along the ice to Monte was nothing short of miraculous. Many started to cheer, forgetting their former antipathy toward the oft maligned girl. Monte passed the puck behind his back to Nancy who was breaking down centre ice, headed for the goal. Despite the clever work of the opposing defence, Nancy skilfully picked up the pass and immediately lifted the puck through the air and it landed right on Myrna's stick as she streaked down the right side. A slight flick of her wrist and the puck sailed into the net. It was 5-1, and the crowd roared their approval.

Monte, Myrna and Nancy enthusiastically hugged one another as their defensemen joyously joined in the celebration. Since the combination had only been on the ice about 20 seconds, Coach Wellman left them on for the ensuing face-off. Again, Nancy managed to get the puck, and this time she hit Myrna with a pin-point pass. Myrna manoeuvred deftly around a defensemen and just as the goalie moved to cut down her angle for a shot, she dropped the puck behind her for the trailing Nancy. That was all it took. Nancy found Monte wide open, as he was skating in on the right side. The goalie was caught completely flat –footed and in 35 seconds, Cree Lake had scored two goals. 5-2 and the fans were on their feet cheering uncontrollably.

Skating off the ice, the three were ecstatic. Meanwhile, their replacements were ready to do battle. Ted lined up for the face off and once again, Cree Lake took control. Another goal scored by a defenseman from the point and with 6 minutes left in the first period, Cree Lake had cut the margin to 5-3.

About three minutes later, speedy defensemen Larry Thundercloud found Hatto Stalking Moon at the centre line and sprung him for a break-away. 5-4 and Coach Wellman was afraid the ice on the lake might crack, because of all the noise being made by the fans.

Many fans were shaking their heads in disbelief at what was happening. Yet, even though she had played a remarkable game, when Nancy skated on the ice with

2:15 left in the period, some in the crowd were spooked by the thought of what might happen. She was constantly being harassed by the Stony Narrows team, who resented a girl being on the ice. How long would she be able to hold her temper? When would she blow? It was only a matter of time, many in the crowd began to think. But it wasn't just Nancy they were concerned about. What about the rest of the team? This team was dynamite waiting to explode.

Yet, the only explosion so far was on the scoreboard, and what was about to occur would be talked about in Cree Lake for years to come, as an explosion of an entirely different kind was about to occur. Coach Wellman, deciding that it was time to take a gamble, put out a line made up of all forwards. Nancy, Myrna and Monte were paired with Hatto Stalking Moon and a towering 206 centimetre (6 feet 9 inches) hulk who tipped the scales at 145 kilos (320 pounds). Grif "Bad Boy" Joe was more a mascot than a player, and at 16, the youngest member of the team. All he asked of Coach Wellman was to simply be on the team, with no expectation that he would ever see a shift on the ice. Yet, Coach Wellman had noticed all first period how enthusiastic Grif was about what was happening on the ice. Every time one of his team-mates would take a cheap shot from the Stony Narrows enforcer, Billy Hitchcock, Grif would pound one fist into the other. Knowing how much the rest of the team respected Grif for his tenacious determination to be on the team, even though his skating abilities were limited, was an inspiration to the coach and the team. Seeing that Hitchcock was on the ice, Wellman looked at Grif and said, "Grif, you're up."

Grif, in apparent shock, replied, "me, coach."

Grinning, Coach Wellman replied, "you Grif."

As the rest of the team looked on in amazement, Grif said, "you sure coach?

Almost laughing out-loud, the coach said, "yes." He continued, "and you only have one job. Don't worry about the puck, just hit Hitchcock. That is your only assignment. Keep him out of the play, and if he comes near one of our players, see he doesn't do any damage. Get out there before we get a penalty for delay of game."

Jumping over the boards enthusiastically, Grif lined up opposite Hitchcock. Assuming something was amiss, Hitchcock wearily backed away from Grif. Grif moved with him. Hitchcock backed further away, and again, Grif moved with him. The referee looked over his shoulder at what was going on and grimaced at the two players. He dropped the puck, and Grif immediately wobbled after Hitchcock who retreated back to the Cree Lake blue line as the puck and the rest of the players moved into the other end of the rink. While the action at the other end was fast and furious, the fans were only watching Grif and Hitchcock play cat and mouse with each other. Grif, trying as hard as he could, but not being as good a skater as Hitchcock, simply was exhausting his bulky body in the pursuit. Finally, Hitchcock circled all the way back behind the Cree Lake net. Cree Lake goalie, Jake Thundercloud, couldn't believe it, as Hitchcock adroitly circled the net with an exhausted Grif in constant pursuit but never able to catch the fleet-footed Hitchcock. Suddenly, there was a celebration at the other end of the ice, as Monte had just scored a goal to tie it 5-5. Grif, seemingly delighted that play had been stopped, waved his right glove at Hitchcock in disdain, gave up the chase and wearily wobbled over to the bench where he got a resounding cheer from the crowd. As he looked at Coach Wellman, breathing heavily from exhaustion, he meekly said, "Coach, I tried, I really tried, but I just couldn't catch him."

The players erupted in laughter and it suddenly dawned on each one of them that they were more than a pack of un-coachable rogues with an attitude problem. They were a team. They were about to prove just how much of a team they were. As the siren went off signalling the end of the first period, they meandered off the ice to the warming hut behind the bench determined to beat Stony Narrows.

Coach Wellman felt that he had a secret weapon that most teams would underrate. That secret weapon was Nancy Running Elk. Her reputation for being volatile had proved unfounded so far in the game, in spite of the fact that she was a primary target for the Stony Narrows team that seemed to resent a girl who was obviously the best skater on the ice. In fact, she reminded the coach of an extremely small player he had seen play in Salt Lake, Utah many years ago. Doug Palazarri had been underestimated by his competition too and the competition learned to regret it.

The coach started the second period with her, Myrna and Monte on the forward line, backed up by Benson Frank and Larry Thundercloud on defence. Although Stony Narrows won the face-off, somehow Nancy wound up with the puck on her skate blade, and immediately kicked a pass to Myrna. Just at that instance, Nancy was levelled with a crushing check from Hitchcock. Her tiny body literally flew across the ice from the force of the blow. Even the most courteous of players will sometimes err in judgment at such times and retaliate for even what might be a legal but nearly lethal blow. Strange to say, Nancy never once caused a penalty to be inflicted on her side, no matter how brutal the Stony Narrows team was with her.

As Nancy careened into the boards, she bounced up instantly and moved forward into the Stony Narrows zone. Streaking behind the net, circling out in front, she saw a blistering shot from Frank who was on the point. She deftly extended her stick about waist high, catching the puck in mid air and directed it upward away from the sprawling goalie who was defenceless in stopping the puck from finding the upper left hand corner of the net. The cheers reverberated all about the rink. What a comeback. It was now 6-5, but the Cree Lake Badgers were not finished. They continued to literally destroy the demoralized Stony Narrows team. With a 12-5 lead and only one minute left in the game, a deafening chant could be heard from the frenzied fans. The chant began: "Grif! Grif! Grif! Grif!" Even the players sitting on the bench looked at Coach Wellman and took up the chant, "Grif! Grif! Grif! Grif!"

The coach looked down the bench, pointed at Grif and said, "your public is calling."

Climbing over the boards onto the ice, Grif seemed to skate more assuredly now. He was not just a mascot. He was genuinely part of the team. Lining up to the right of Nancy, who was at centre, preparing to take the face-off, Grif had a look of grim determination. On the right wing, Ted Ironchest took his index glove finger and pointed back to the defensemen, Larry Thundercloud and Benson

Frank. Then he pointed to Grif, as if to say that he was the one who should be set-up for the goal.

Nancy, looking out of the corner of her eye, knew what was up. No one would score unless it was Grif. This was his moment. When the puck was dropped, she got the back of her blade on it and was able to pull it back to Frank on right defence. He made a hard pass to Ted, who swiftly put it on Nancy's stick as she was all alone streaking toward the Stony Narrows blue line. She picked up the pass without breaking stride and left two players in their tracks, as she was on a wide-open breakaway. There was no way she could not score. This would be an easy goal.

Meanwhile, Grif was wobbling determinedly right behind Nancy, taking long strides to try and catch up to her without much success.

Expecting a blistering shot from Nancy, the fans all jumped to their feet. That was when they all gasped with surprise. The goalie moved to his right in an attempt to stop what was a sure goal, and Nancy simply dropped the puck behind her and left it for Grif to glide into the left hand bottom of the net. Pandemonium broke lose in the stands, on the ice and on the Cree Lake bench. Grif, dear Grif, the most improbable of goal scorers, had just put one into the net, courtesy of the unselfish play of Nancy and her line mates. The Cree Lake Badgers were a team.

CHAPTER 5
WHY COULDN'T HE BLOT THEM OUT?

The second game that weekend was not as thrilling. The Badgers new found team work was just too much for the bewildered Stony Narrows team. The contest wasn't even close, the Badgers winning 7-0.

Sunday morning, the few people in town who went to church service were more interested in talking about the hockey game after services than the message the Reverend Johnson had tried to convey. The whole village was abuzz with talk of Nancy, Myrna, Monte and the rest of the lads who had made the town so proud. Then there was that final scoring play when good old Grif was the recipient of the most unselfish play anyone could ever remember seeing. Yet, there was something sinister that few people knew about in the early morning, but Monte was about to find out about it.

"Monte, you heard the news yet?"

With these abrupt words Ted burst upon his pal, who was, as usual, spending Sunday morning flipping a puck at a hockey goal he had drawn on the side of his mother's storage shed.

Monte turned to look at his friend. It was plain to be seen that Ted was labouring under considerable excitement. His face was flushed as if with running, while his eyes glowed much more than usual under ordinary conditions and he was gasping for breath.

"Why, no, I haven't heard a thing, but obviously, I am about to, or you will burst a gut."

47

"You won't believe it.. It was a regular down-right burglary that was pulled off, even if the stuff taken consisted of candy, cigarettes, and the like, as well as some sporting goods and several rifles that were locked on a gun rack."

"I assume it was the general store and grocery that was robbed."

"You got it buddy and big time. Hey, we haven't had this much excitement since the town found out Nancy got pregnant." The last statement kind of stuck in Ted's throat, as he realized he shouldn't have mentioned that, especially now that he and Monte were her team-mates. You could tell by his expression he regretted saying it, but it was too late to take it back. Monte just sort of grimaced and let it pass.

Trying to wax over what he had said, Ted continued. "Constable McMillan says he has a good idea who it was, and that he could put his hands on them pretty quick."

"Yeah, and I am sure he figures one of them is Nancy," Monte said as a troubled look crept across his face.

"Sure thing," continued Ted, shrugging his shoulders. "When someone has built a nefarious reputation along those lines like Nancy has, it is likely that people will immediately place the blame on those who have caused trouble in the past.

"How did you happen to hear about it, Ted?"

"Oh! I chanced to be out early this morning on an errand for mother, and passing through the public square on my way back I saw a crowd around the store. I hung around for awhile and heard all sorts of things. But Monte, they've got one of the thieves, already."

"So, who was it got arrested?"

"Nancy's old boyfriend, Lenny Dan."

"McMillan found a bandana belonging to Dan in the alleyway behind the store and he made a b-line to Lenny's house and insisted on making a thorough search of the entire grounds. After not even bothering to search the house, he looked under the floor of the barn and found some of the stuff that was taken: candy, cigarettes, two of the rifles, and even a pair of high priced hockey skates."

"What did Lenny say when they found the stolen stuff hidden under his barn floor?" further questioned Monte.

"Nary a thing would he say, except to declare himself innocent, and that he himself had heard a noise out there last night, and guessed that some enemy of his must have set up a mean game on him, wanting to get him nabbed. Then, McMillan pulled seven packs of cigarettes out of a nearby coffee can, every one of them the very brand that was stolen."

"It looks pretty bad for Lenny," remarked Monte.

"Yeah, I guess so."

"But what about the other thief, Ted?"

"Well, McMillan said there wasn't any doubt that it must be Nancy, and it would just be a matter of time until her old boyfriend would rat her out. He went immediately to her house and over the protestations of her grandmother, handcuffed her and brought her in for questioning. I was down by the lockup when he showed up with Nancy in tow, and acted like he had just caught public enemy number one. He really has it in for Nancy, always has."

"But you have never seen such a cool customer as Nancy. She smiled brazenly in the face of the constable. She was waving at the crowd and walked right into jail with her head held high. They searched her grandmother's place from top to bottom and found not even a scrap of the stolen goods."

"Well, what happened next?"

"McMillan declared that Nancy had only been smarter than her ex-boyfriend in hiding the spoils where no one could find them. He told her he would have to arrest her on general suspicion, because she and Lenny were known to still hang around with each other, even though they had supposedly broken up. In fact, they were seen whispering something to each other right after the hockey match Saturday night. Obviously, they were planning to rob the general store."

"O.K., and what did Nancy say to that?" asked Monte.

"Would you believe it, Monte, she up and told Constable McMillan without even losing her temper that she had an iron-glad alibi. You see, the robbery was done before eleven o'clock last night, because a clock that was knocked down when the thieves were rummaging around in the store. It had been broken, and it stopped at just a quarter to eleven."

50

Monte actually thought for a second, and wondered who her alibi might be. Was she with some guy? Then, he thought to himself, why should I care who she was with just as he blurted out "but how about Nancy's alibi? Who was it?"

Shaking his head, Ted said nonchalantly, "you won't believe it."

"I'll believe it. It was probably her grandmother. Yeah, like McMillan is going to believe that Nancy couldn't have slipped out without her grandmother knowing about it. Everybody in town knows she has slipped out for years. I even remember when she was nine years old and used to get caught summers swimming in the lake at midnight."

"Oh! Nancy had much better proof than her grandmother, Monte. She demanded that the constable call up Dan Wilton."

Shocked that Nancy would be with a man of nearly 60 that late at night by herself, Monte proclaimed, "you've got to be kidding. She was with Dan Wilton? I hope Wilton's wife was also with her."

"Well, where else would Wilton's wife be? You ever seen her when she wasn't with Dan? Seems Nancy slipped over there, but nobody is revealing the reason she was there. The point is that Dan Wilton and his wife both say she was there. Alibi confirmed. As for what she was doing over there. The Wilton's said it was none of McMillan's business. She was there, and that confirmed her alibi. If that wasn't good enough, old man Wilton said he would call up Regina and have a real high-powered attorney come out and see to things. McMillan backed off, then."

Monte let out a satisfied grin. At least Nancy had not been with some guy. There were those thoughts again, dancing about his brain. Why couldn't he get Nancy off his mind? Why did he keep visualizing that mischievous smile and those dark, dancing, sparkling eyes? Seeming to come out of a trance Monte proclaimed, "and what did McMillan do then?"

"He still desperately wanted to arrest her, but what could he do? She had an alibi and Lenny Dan was still proclaiming he had been framed. It was really funny when Nancy told McMillan that if he didn't get off her back, she was going to contact the Human Rights Commission and have them send a contingent of monitors out here to see how the police were discriminating against First Nations people."

Ted entusiastically continued. "McMillan said he knew Nancy was involved, even if she had managed to cover her tracks so cunningly; and even fool Dan Wilton, but she hadn't fooled him. He told her he'd let her go temporarily, but that the investigation was only beginning."

Monte felt indignant over Nancy's tribulations. After all, she was his team-mate and he believed in her. As he looked out his window, contemplating the events of the past several hours in the sleepy little part of the world he called home, there were those visions of Nancy and that crooked little alluring smile that would always slowly creep across her face. Why did those visions keep cropping up in his mind. Why couldn't he blot them out?

CHAPTER 6
MONTE HAD NEVER BEEN SO CONFUSED

Coming out of his near trance-like state, Monte turned to Ted and said, "you feel like taking a walk, Ted?"

"All right," said Ted. "This mysterious case of Nancy Running Elk have something to do with our walk?"

"Of course not Ted, we can always use a little exercise, and who knows, we might walk as far as Dan Wilton's place."

Ted looked interested. "So, that's the way it is, uh?" he remarked. ""You want to question Mr. Wilton. You certainly seem to have taken an awful lot of interest in Nancy lately."

"I mean only to ask a few questions that will clear up a little point that is a bit muddled for me. After all, Nancy is our team-mate, and we are supposed to stick together aren't we?"

Ted, somewhat concerned about his friend's interest in a girl whom they both had great disdain for only a few days ago was rather blunt with a comment. "Yeah, this sticking business is fine, but I am beginning to wonder just how close you want to stick to Nancy."

Monte, shrugging his shoulders, gave Ted a stern look. "Listen, I just want to understand why Nancy was out at the Wilton's so late last night."

"So, you think she knew about the planned burglary, and she just wanted to make sure she had an alibi?"

Monte got up, motioned for Ted to follow him and shortly afterwards the pair were trudging along the road toward the Wilton's place. On the way, they met a car coming down the road from the Wilton's. It was Constable McMillan. He nodded to the boys as he zipped past.

After a short time, they arrived at the Wilton's, where Dan was tending to some flowers in the front yard while his wife sat on the porch shivering in a rocking chair. Dan Wilton was a big man, but age had apparently withered what was once a very muscular and powerful body. His "poor old wife," as the town referred to her, was a shrivelled up and dishevelled woman who looked 80 rather than 60. She never smiled and always seemed to be carrying a heavy burden in a heart that had, no doubt, been broken by troubles that seemed overwhelming. However, they were both known as kind souls who always were willing to lend a helping hand to those in need, even though, they themselves, seemed more in need than most.

Stopping his gardening, Dan Wilton welcomed the boys and asked them to have a seat on the porch with him and his wife. Mrs. Wilton nodded hello to the boys, but seemed too deep in thought to converse with them.

Monte plunged into the matter without waste of time. He asked Wilton if he had seen the weekend hockey games, and Wilton intonated that even though he had not seen them, he had heard about all the excitement from several people, including Nancy Running Elk.

This led naturally to Monte asking if he had heard about the robbery at the general store. Answering in the affirmative, Wilton continued by saying, "and Constable McMillan was just here to ask me about the incident."

"Yeah, I figured that when we saw him pass us on the road, because the rumour is that you are Nancy Running Elk's alibi, which she will certainly need, because McMillan has always been out to get her."

"Well, that is true, Nancy was here with us. We can both attest to that," he said, as he looked over at Mrs. Wilton, nodded and continued, "eh, honey."

Monte continued the conversation with a profession of his belief in Nancy's total innocence. Mr. Wilton nodded in agreement and professed loudly, "rest assured she is entirely innocent of the crime. I have known Nancy for many years. She has had a bad name and a bad reputation, it is true; but somehow I have always known that there are elements of great good in her, if only people would give her a chance."

Now came the tricky part of the conversation, as Monte tried to muster up the courage to ask what he really wanted to know, even though it was really none of his business. "There was one thing I wanted to learn, sir, if you don't mind telling me about it. It concerns her being out here last night. Is she usually prone to come out here on Saturday nights?"

Mr. Wilton smiled, and said, "up to now it has always been on Monday nights Nancy came by. That was more convenient for us, as a rule, and she accommodated herself to our wishes. But yesterday afternoon before the game, she dropped in to see us, with her skates dangling across his shoulder and her hockey bag in her hand. She said she would like very much to come by Saturday night, instead of Monday; and that she had a good reason for making the change, which meant a whole lot to her for a reason I don't know."

Well, Monte knew now that Nancy must have known about the plans to burglarize the general store, but he was still curious as to why Nancy was a regular visitor to the farm.

"I see," remarked Monte; "and it was clever of Nancy. You agreed, of course, sir, seeing that she was here last night?"

"It made no particular difference to us," added Mr. Wilton, "and I was glad to know the girl cared enough about her time with us to want to make the change. So I told her to be along as usual about seven. She was here until 11:15."

"You remember that positively then, sir, the hour, I mean?" asked Monte. He had to fight back the urge to ask him just what Nancy was doing out at the farm once a week.

"Oh! I could swear to it," came the reply. "In the first place I heard our mantel clock strike eleven, and counted the strokes myself, remarking that it was late and she needed to get home so her grandmother would not worry about her. She asked of she could have a cup of hot chocolate before going to warm her body up for the 10 minute walk home and Alice made us all a cup. We sipped on it until 11:15 when she left. I don't like the idea of her having known about the robbery, and keeping silent, but I know her as an honourable person, and she just may have felt duty bound not to rat on her friends. I can kind of understand that, even though it was wrong."

So their interview with Mr. Wilton proved a very enjoyable one after all. Monte felt he should like to know the big amiable Mr. Wilton better, for he was obviously a truly kind person. His entire demeanour exuded a caring person, indeed. Yet, still he wished that he knew a good way to broach the reasons for Nancy's weekly visits. Well, no need to spoil a nice conversation by appearing to be too inquisitive. Thoughts of Nancy danced in his head once again, as he and Ted got up and left. What was making him think so much about Nancy? Monte had never been so confused.

CHAPTER 7
GUILTY, JUST AS SUSPECTED

"Do you know," mused Ted, as they continued on their way to town, "the more I learn about Nancy, the more I think we have all terribly misjudged her over the years. Maybe she isn't as bad as we think she is. After all, we arc not saints ourselves. So judging other people's actions might not be very appropriate for us."

"I was just going to say that myself," Monte told him. "There is something about her though that is mysterious. I just wish I had the nerve to come out and ask the Wilton's why she comes to see them once a week? It's not like they were related or something. Nobody is really friends with the Wilton's, even though they are respected all over town. They just aren't the real friendly type. So, what is with Nancy and them?"

Ted turned to Monte and said, "you don't think it has anything to do with their son disappearing three years ago do you?"

Quizzically, Monte responded. "Well, I wouldn't think so. I know that was when old Mrs. Wilton seemed to fall apart even more than usual. She used to be pretty lively until her son just up and left home. I don't know why you would get upset about a 35 year old son leaving home. I'd say that he was long overdue."

Laughing, Ted exclaimed, "yeah, could you see your mom or mine getting upset about us leaving home? They'd probably pack our bags for us, open the door and give us a swift kick in the behind as we were going out the door."

Monte, rather philosophically, said, "well, if you had two trouble makers like us for sons, wouldn't you be happy to see them leave home?"

Laughing together, they continued to amble down the road to town, when, for some reason, Ted's thoughts wondered back to the Wilton's son. "Wonder why their son never came back. I hear he has never even written them a letter. Apparently, they have no idea where he is. It was as if James Wilton just dropped out of sight one day. And so the years have rolled by and apparently all Mrs. Wilton does is sit in her rocker on the front porch or in the recliner by the living room window in the house, sorrowfully waiting for her son to return, always gazing up the road, expecting her boy to show up."

Monte was greatly moved by the sad tale, which, however, he knew could be easily matched in every town and city in the country. Pain and loneliness were a common malady of humankind, no matter where you lived.

"How sad," mused Monte, with a shake of his head; "and to think that poor old lady is eternally watching and yearning for her boy to come back. It is all she lives for, to see her son again."

Ted, in a heavy-hearted manner, said, "yeah, and poor old Mr. Wilton has to deal with that every day of his life. It must be just as difficult for him, because you know he misses his son, too. Of course, I don't know why anyone would miss James Wilton. He was a bigger terror than we are, and he was old enough to know better. Remember when he beat up Arlene French in the old tavern outside of town? And what about the time they shipped him off for trial down in Prince Albert? That was for robbing a tourist in Finch Lake? They showed up at the Wilton farm and he nearly killed Constable Givens before they were able to arrest him."

"Yeah, I remember that they said the victim and the witnesses were so intimidated by him that they refused to testify. All they could do was get him for assaulting an officer, but they threw that case out, because they said there was no proof he had done anything wrong since the victim and witnesses refused to verify it was him who did the robbery, and the police had no business going onto the farm without a formal complaint or warrant. He just sauntered back into town as high and mighty as you please, like nothing had even happened. If you ask me, his Mom and Dad were lucky he left town. He certainly hasn't been missed by nobody but his parents."

Monte couldn't believe what was about to come out of his mouth. "Yeah, but he is their son, no matter how bad he is. Hey, we've done some pretty terrible things in our lives, but our Moms have always stood by us. In your case, even your Dad has put up with a lot of your shenanigans. Although, he certainly isn't as tolerant as your Mom."

"Yeah, I guess you are right Monte. Love is a funny thing isn't it? You never know who you are going to love. When you are going to love. Sometimes, you don't even know why you love someone."

That last statement really got to Monte. Yeah, he thought to himself, sometimes you don't know why you love someone. And there it was again, visions of Nancy dancing in his head.

So the two chums continued to talk all the way back to town. Monte and Ted seemed to have matured a great deal the past few days. They both felt it, but never brought it up to each other. There was something different about them, now. Even their stride down the road was not as cocky or malevolent as it had been in prior days. Funny that they were both thinking the same thing at the same time. Had the words of Coach Wellman made them realize that there was always a chance for a fresh start, a chance to change even though people didn't think you could.

That Monday in school, the talking in the halls was all about the exciting games over the weekend, and how the coming weekend, the team was journeying down to Sandy Lake for a two game series.

On Tuesday afternoon, Ted and Monte saw Dan Wilton in town coming out of the general store. They were about to wave to him, when Nancy came up to Mr. Wilton, and they walked down the street together. Nancy seemed to be whispering something, and Mr. Wilton kept shaking his head up and down, as if he was agreeing with whatever she was saying. At the end of town, they parted company, Nancy walking left toward the rink and hockey practice, no doubt, and Mr. Wilton up the road toward his farm.

At practice, Coach Wellman told them that it was foolish to rest on their laurels. That, yes, they had played a terrific game, and really came together as a team, but that was only two games of a 36 game season. If they wanted to be successful there were three things they had to do. First and most foremost, he would expect to see report cards at the end of every grading period. If the grades were not up-to-par, a player could face dismissal from the team. He did not expect all A's, but he did expect maximum effort. Second, the team had to always remember that regardless of what the scoreboard read at the end of a game, as long as they gave it their maximum effort, they would never be losers. Finally, the coach made it plain that they would always play as a team. There was no one indispensable player, any more than there was no indispensable coach.

At the end of his statement about no indispensable coach, he said, "I take that back. The coach is indispensable. There is no way you guys can get by without me."

The team laughed together, and realized that their coach was more than just a coach, he was their friend. He was someone who would have their backs. He respected them as players and as individuals. It was something they all craved, and they finally had it from someone who was not there to judge them. This was a team, a team moulded together by mutual respect and admiration. This was not just about hockey. It was about life and all its possibilities for those willing to make the sacrifices required. Success was not judged by the size of a bank account, by the job you had, by the home you lived in or the car you drove. Success was feeling a part of something bigger than yourself. Success was knowing you had people who cared for you and for whom you cared. Success was knowing your true worth as an individual who was free of judgemental arrogance and greed.

Coach Wellman could see in the sparking eyes gazing at him, as they seemed to hang on his every word, that these young people were going to be a formidable force. This was a team of destiny.

That weekend they beat Sandy Lake 7-0 and 5-0. Suddenly, the hockey team had a prominent place in the conversations that were carried on wherever two or more Cree Lake citizens clustered. As Coach Wellman's wife Janice tended to her patients, they were more interested in hearing about what the coach thought about the team's chances of winning the Provincial Championship, maybe even going all the way to Nationals, than their illnesses.

Meanwhile the mystery concerning that robbery had not yet been wholly solved. Lenny Dan still languished in the lock-up down at the jail, his folks having been unable to secure bail for him due to their dire financial situation. Since they could not raise the amount themselves, there seemed to be no person in the whole community philanthropically inclined enough to take chances with Lenny, who was reckoned an exceedingly slippery and devious individual, who would most likely run away before his trial came off, leaving his bondsman to "hold the bag," as most people put it. Unfortunately for Lenny, he had just turned 18, so he was no longer considered a juvenile, and he would have to face an indictment in adult court for the first time in his life.

He was just as stubborn as ever in his denial of complicity in the robbery. Doubtless, Lenny believed that a lie well stuck to was the best course of action. He was scared, but not scared enough to rat out any friends. Anyway, Constable McMillan was not a man with whom you could negotiate. He loved locking people up, and would never make a deal just to get the other culprit. Anyway, how solid was the evidence? The answer was "pretty solid." He had been caught with the goods on him. All that loot hidden under the old barn at his place was positive proof of his guilt. Still, he held out, and declared himself the victim of some base plot calculated to ruin his reputation; which was rather a queer thing for Lenny to say, since the only reputation he had was as a lying, trouble-making thief.

Constable McMillan still had a strong hunch that Nancy was involved, because she was never far from any trouble that cropped up in Cree Lake. In fact, he thought it didn't matter even if she wasn't involved. She had gotten away with plenty of misdeeds, so even if she was innocent of this particular crime, she deserved to be locked up anyway for all the other crimes she had probably committed. Although she had never been caught for any major felonious misdeed, her reputation for defying authority was justification enough for McMillan to constantly try to catch her for any minor infraction of the law.

Then there was the other suspect who was prominently on McMillan's radar, Tipper Running Bear. He had even gone to Tipper's humble shack on the edge of town and made a thorough search, high and low, but without the least success. If Tipper were guilty. he must have been smarter than his confederate, who had hidden his share of the plunder under the loose boards of the floor of his folks' barn.

Not having any evidence beyond suspicion, the officer did not dare arrest Tipper Running Bear, who continued to loaf about his customary corners in town and look impudently at every fellow who glared at him when passing. Monte, himself, never once doubted the guilt of Tipper Running Bear; though he fancied the authorities might have a hard time catching him, unless the stubborn Lenny at the very last, finding himself on the way to prison, confessed, and implicated his companion or companions.

Monte and Ted were talking about that very same thing one afternoon while on the way home from hockey practice. "Where do you think Tipper could have hidden the stuff," Ted asked.

"Oh! there would be plenty of places, and no one is likely to ever run across it, because Tipper is a lot smarter than his buddy Lenny. I never could figure out why a smart girl like Nancy would have anything to do with those two miscreants. She is an independent sort, and much too smart to get hooked up with those guys. It seems she has made some bad choices for friends ever since she got pregnant."

Ted, laughingly said, "yeah, now Nancy has us and the rest of the team for friends. She has really come up in the world."

Monte replied, "you got that right. We are the cream of the crop. That is one lucky girl, now." Oops, there was that vision of Nancy dancing in his mind again.

"My guess is old Tipper won't be able to keep himself away from his cache," Monte continued, as he struggled to get that image of Nancy out of his head. "That may be his undoing. You know, when an ordinary thief has done something big, and is being looked for, the smart police always ask whether he has a wife or a sweetheart; because they know that sooner or later he is bound to communicate with such a person, and so a clue may be found to his hiding-place. Well, Tipper's heart will be located where his treasure is. He'll soon get a yearning to indulge in some of the candy and cigarettes he's got hidden away. Especially the cigarettes. He smokes like a chimney on a cold winter night. One thing about us, we may not follow the rules the way people think we should, but we certainly are smart enough to know cigarettes are nothing but an addictive drug pedalled by corporate criminals."

Ted, smiling at his friend's political homily replied with a question. "When did you get to be a philosopher and protector of the economically disadvantaged?

"Well Ted, I have been listening to a lot of what the coach has said about the powerful and rich not wanting people like us to succeed on the ice or in life, because they need us as their slaves to work in their sweat shops for paltry wages. You know, he is more than our coach. I think he really believes that if he can reach just a few of us with his ideas about fighting for justice that maybe one or two of us can make a difference in the world."

Ted, taking what Monte said to heart, became a bit more serious in his manner. "Yeah, I get the idea coach actually believes we are capable of changing things if we just get off our butts and stop feeling sorry for ourselves and fight against those who want to keep us mired in economic servitude."

Monte, laughing out loud, said, "now, who is being philosophical. We need to get back to what should be done to make Tipper fess up to the crime and finally totally exonerate Nancy."

Monte continued, "say what you want about the motives of Constable McMillan, he is a thorough cop. My bet is that he is keeping an eye on Tipper. I am no fan of Constable McMillan, and somehow I hate to have a hand in railroading Tipper into jail. It's true he ought to be there, for he's a terror to the whole community; but he's got a mother, Ted, and I'd hate to see her swollen eyes, and remember that I'd had a hand in parting her from her boy. It isn't as if I were paid for doing such things, as McMillan is; this is hardly any business of mine. Anyway, remember how Mrs. Wilton pines for her boy day and night, and he was a bigger rogue than Tipper. I would sure hate to see Mrs. Running Bear wind up like Mrs. Wilton, sitting there in her hut, looking out the window, waiting for her boy."

"Well now, somehow I don't just look at it the way you do, Monte. Perhaps I'm not quite so tender-hearted as you are. I know the children of the rich get probation while those of us with much less get carted off to jail, but sometimes there is some justice, and Tipper is a guy I'd like to see suffer the consequences. I hate to say it, but it is true. That guy is a menace. Also, how about Nancy?"

"Nancy is our team-mate Ted. If a team-mate needs help, we give it to them, but we don't support them in crime. Yet, I do not believe Nancy had anything to do with this. So far, Nancy seems to have turned over a new leaf and is minding her own business. In fact, I think we all misjudged her for years, not because she did anything bad, but because she got pregnant at 14, and most people were always badmouthing her without any real proof of what she had done. Name one thing we know for a fact that she did that was bad. OK, she got pregnant, but other than that, everything we hear is innuendo and gossip. Then she hangs out with the wrong people on occasion, and we all assume that also means she is bad. Who else does she have to hang-out with when the rest of us here shun her. No, I refuse to believe Nancy was involved. I do know there is something mysterious about her. That I fully grant, but I refuse to believe bad of her. I absolutely refuse."

Ted, always a bit curious about how intense Monte was when it came to Nancy, decided to change the subject a bit. "Well, one thing I will have to admit. That girl can sure play hockey."

"You got that right, dude. If we keep playing like we have the first four games, we are going to put Cree Lake on the hockey map, and Nancy Running Elk and Myrna St. John will have a lot to do with it."

Ted, realizing that the two girls on the team had made a really big difference in the team's success, said, "yeah, I was dead set against having one girl on the team, much less two, but I have to give Coach Wellman credit. He knows raw talent when he sees it. Next week, Regina is in town, and I would hate to face them without Nancy and Myrna on the team."

Just then, Grif came running up the road as excited as a teenager who had just gotten his first kiss. Huffing and puffing wildly, he was greeted by Monte with some humorous words. "Hey, Ted, it is Cree Lake's renown scorer and fan favourite, Grif Bad Boy Joe."

Shaking his head furiously, Grif replied, "you're just jealous because I am Nancy's favourite target for a pass. I got more ability than any of you guys. That's why she knows my stick will be right where it is supposed to be when she makes a pass. I hear the Winnipeg Jets will probably have a scout out here to check me out any day, now."

As Grif turned with the boys and they started walking to town together, Ted offered another comment. "Yeah, and you are also the most modest player on the team."

"Hey, if you two can stop being jealous of my superior hockey talents for awhile, I have something to tell you, and is it big. I have discovered the goods on Tipper Running Bear. No doubt at all – he is guilty, just as suspected."

CHAPTER 8
DON'T WORRY, MOMMY WILL BE ALRIGHT

"Tell us about it, Grif, please; since you've got us excited by the news."

"Well, I guess you noticed the best player on the team, me, was not at practice today. But it wasn't any fault of mine, I give you my word. I had to do something at the behest of Constable McMillan."

All this was said with such a lugubrious expression that Monte could not help but smile. Grif was joking about being the best player, as he always liked to be sardonic, and he always had such a unique way of being self-deprecating that you sometimes had a difficult time of telling when he was serious.

"It's plain to be seen you started on this walk feeling you had something important to tell us, Grif," Monte went on to remark. "Of course you realize it was not much of a practice today without your superior skills there for us to admire so much. However, now might be a good time to tell us what was so important that we were denied the privilege of your company in practice today."

"Just this, Monte. Constable McMillan sent me out to deliver a package to the Upton place. Said it was terribly important that it get there right away." Then, almost as an afterthought, Grif got a quizzical look on his face and interrupted his train-of-thought with another comment. "Funny thing, I was walking out to the Upton's and McMillan sped by me like a mad-man. Wonder why he didn't just take the package to the Upton's if he was going that direction anyway?"

70

Getting a bit perturbed with Grif's wandering mind, Ted said, "back on the subject please, Grif. You were telling us about knowing that Tipper was in cahoots with Lenny."

"Yeah! Yeah? That's right. So, anyway, I was well out of town, and walking briskly along." There it was again. Grif's mind was wandering. He was silent and in deep thought.

"Grif! Oh Grif! Earth to Grif! Come in Grif," sarcastically said Monte, as he shook his head in frustration.

"Oh, sorry guys. I was just thinking that McMillan came roaring back toward town. Waved at me again and shouted out the window to get the package to the Upton's fast. Still can't figure out why he didn't just deliver it. Anyway, I got to the Upton's in about another minute and who is working there in the Upton's yard, but Tipper. And what do you think he was doing?"

Getting a bite exasperated, Monte said, "hey, Grif, I have no idea. You are the one who is telling the story. You going to finish it before Christmas?"

"Yeah, sure," said Grif, rather sarcastically and giggling like a kid who had just been handed a lollipop. "I'll get it told by Halloween – guaranteed."

Monte and Ted were both getting frustrated, but they had known Grif long enough to realize that he had his own unique way of doing everything. They decided to just shut up and let him tell the story his way, no matter how long it took.

"Anyway, I was thinking about Friday and Saturday's games against Regina. We are gonna win, no doubt about it. If coach gives me a shift with Nancy, I'll get a goal."

Both Monte and Ted were beginning to wonder just how long this would go on, when Grif finally got to the point, almost. "Anyway, Tipper was smoking a cigarette." Then Grif got that look again, and went in a completely different direction. "Nasty habit that smoking, can't figure out why any kid would be dumb enough to do it. You know, even my parents were smart enough to quit after smoking nearly 25 years. Turned out to be smarter than I thought they were."

Monte, frustrated to the point of almost screaming, said, "Grif, please. We agree with you, smoking is dumb, but right now we want to hear about Tipper."

"Yeah! Anyway Tipper was puffing away, blowing smoke right in my face." Then there Grif went again, drifting off to La La Land. "You would think he'd know that second hand smoke is bad for people. Don't know why so many people are so rude that they will smoke around you and make you get cancer, too. Inconsiderate I'd say. Just down-right inconsiderate. You know what really burns me up? Seeing parents pushing baby carriages while they are puffing away on a cigarette. That's child abuse, pure and simple. Yeah, child abuse is what it is."

In total frustration, Ted pleaded with Grif. "Please, please tells us the rest of your story. What about Tipper?"

"Yeah, if you guys would stop interrupting me, I'd finish the tale. So, Tipper gives me a nasty look, as he is puffing away, sighs a bit, flips the cigarette right at my feet and walks around to the Upton's back yard without saying a word. I am standing there with the package, so I take it up to the door and the Upton's acted surprised when I told them it was from McMillan. They thanked me and I left."

Seemingly exhausted from his exhortation, Grif took a deep breath, held it for a second, let it out slowly and methodically and continued. "So, I am walking back out the front gate, and I think to myself, wonder what brand of cigarette that was that Tipper threw away. So, I didn't have much trouble. There it was by the gate, right where he threw it. I picked it up and continued on my way." With that Grif took something from his pocket, carefully wrapped in the folds of his handkerchief. It turned out to be a half-smoked cigarette. Monte fastened his eyes instantly on some small printing in blue ink, giving the name of the manufacturer down in Virginia. That was it – Chesterfields. The same brand that was stolen in bulk from the General Store.

"It's the same make as those found under the Lenny's barn-floor," Monte said impressively; "and that alone would be proof that Tipper has a cache somewhere back along the road, perhaps in a hollow tree in the woods. A clever police officer could easily find it by following Tipper."

Somewhat impressed with his acumen as a detective, Grif said, "I myself happen to know his left shoe has a triangular patch across the toe,—that would serve to identify the tracks anywhere. All you do is just follow those tracks in the dirt and you will find his cache. This guy is caught."

"Listen to that, will you, Monte?" gasped the wondering Ted as he got a contemplative look on his face. "If my chum here doesn't take up the line of an investigator of crime for a livelihood, believe me there'll be a great loss to the world. This dude is the modern Sherlock Holmes. What a choice he has to make. A career as an incredible hockey player bringing fans to their feet, or a career bringing criminals to justice."

Monte laughed in a restrained way, as he went on to say, "You are being sarcastic Ted, but our friend here was mighty lucky that McMillan sent him out to the Upton's. Now the question is what will you do about it, Grif, let the constable know of your discovery, or forever hold your peace?"

"Why, I look at it this way," said Grif, with a line of perplexity marked upon his usually smooth forehead, "if it was only a suspicion I might keep quiet, not wanting to injure Tipper, though I've got little cause to love the brute. But since I actually know something that would prove a valuable clue to the officers, I'm afraid it would be what I've heard a lawyer call compounding a felony, if I refused to inform on Tipper. How about that, Monte? I want to do the right thing, even if I hate to be an informer. Also, I am tired of McMillan still trying to accuse Nancy of being involved. Nancy is being unjustly accused, so maybe if the real culprits were caught, McMillan would finally leave Nancy alone."

"It's up to you, Grif, and your duty is plain enough," said Monte.

"Then I ought to see Constable McMillan, you mean?" asked Grif.

"I'd advise you to do so, for your future peace of mind, if nothing else," Monte told the hesitating Grif.

Grif thereupon drew a long breath, and remarked, "I'm more than half sorry now I went back to look for this cigarette; because only for my picking up such positive evidence I needn't get into this nasty game. But I'm in now, and I'll have to shoulder my share of the responsibility, I guess. So, while the thing is still fresh in my mind, I'll trot around to see McMillan. Things have come to a pretty pass here when boys have to lend a helping hand to the police force so as to nab a thief. I never thought I'd stoop so low as to help the police."

With that, Grif bid them a kind adieu with a flick of his waving right wrist and left. When he had a duty to perform, however unpleasant it might be, Grif was accustomed to grappling with it and not compromising.

Ted looked over at Monte and remarked, "How queer things do come about, Monte. Just to think of Grif discovering Tipper sauntering around the Upton's and smoking one of those stolen cigarettes. Pretty stupid of him. I suppose it'll wind up with Tipper being locked up with Lenny, and eventually going to prison this time. I do feel sorry for his mother, though, because it makes me think of poor old Mrs. Wilton and what she goes through every day."

"Few people will be sorry," observed Monte, although he felt a twinge of regret when his mind reverted to their mothers.

"I wonder what Nancy thinks of it all," mused Ted. "She must realize that she has had a narrow escape."

As they had arrived at the point where their paths diverged, the two chums separated. Monte headed for home. He flopped down on his bed and promptly fell into a deep sleep. A couple of hours later, as he was coming out of his slumber, there it was again, visions of Nancy dancing about in his mind.

Usually people like to linger on the ice until long after the shades of night have softly settled down and time for dinner is perilously near. With a jolly bonfire blazing on the bank near the rink, and the skaters going and coming all the while, the prospect is so alluring that it is indeed difficult for any young person to break away from the freedom that is offered on the ice. And the father who has not forgotten his own shortcomings of long ago, when he, too, was irresistibly drawn to the ice, is apt to wisely overlook some such transgression of parental authority, when the ice beckons, and, in spite of good intentions, all outdoors seems to grip a fellow in fetters of steel. Knowing the propensity for lingering at the rink, sometime around 10:00 o'clock, Monte addled down to the frozen surface, and although he didn't realize it, he was subconsciously hoping to see Nancy there, as she was known to go down late at night, so she could skate by herself and practice her end-to-end sprints. Monte still couldn't understand why he kept thinking about Nancy. It definitely wasn't a romantic interest he kept telling himself. After all, she was a mother with a two year old child. Anyway, Monte had plenty of girls prettier than Nancy interested in him. O.K., granted, after thinking her a jerk and malcontent for years, he had discovered she was really a nice person, but that was it – wasn't it? Sure it was, but then why was he disappointed when she wasn't at the rink. He felt the cold all about him, as he forlornly walked back home.

He had on a heavy wool-lined pea-jacket that buttoned close up under his chin and Monte found nothing to complain about in that cold atmosphere, for his blood coursed through his veins with all the richness of healthy youth. As he slowly walked back toward home, he passed the Francis shanty and through a dingy window, a lone lamp could be seen. The world is unevenly divided he thought, some have too much for their own good, and others far too little for comfort. The Francis family had far too little. Yes, they got a government stipend, but with a bevy of genetic illnesses plaguing the household, they had always had a hard time keeping their heads above water.

Monte was about half-way home when something occurred to excite him not a little, though at the time he did not even suspect what an intimate relation it might have in connection with certain facts that he and his chum had only recently been discussing at length.

He saw a wavering figure moving rapidly toward him in the dark. Then Monte discovered, greatly to his surprise, that it was Nancy, and that she held by the hand, her child, Jasmine.

As she approached, he caught himself getting unusually euphoric. His blood seemed to pump through his body faster, and he felt a lump in his throat. Why? Why did this happen every time he was near Nancy?

She tried to speak to him, but seemed overcome with weakness. She reached out her right hand, just as her daughter looked up quizzically at Monte. As she begin to fall forward, Monte reached out and caught her in his arms. He partially lifted her as she said, "he hit me and scared Jasmine. He hit me so hard." She then faded into unconsciousness.

As Jasmine cried uncontrollably, Monte picked up the diminutive Nancy, and carried her toward town. With Jasmine wobbling along on her little legs, Monte could not walk very fast for fear of leaving her behind, but he kept telling her, "don't worry, Mommy will be alright."

CHAPTER 9
WHY WAS HE FOLLOWING COACH WELLMAN

In small Canadian communities, doctors are often only flown in for consultations a few days a month. For that reason, there is usually what is called a Physician's Assistant or Nurse Practitioner who handles most medical emergencies. Janice Wellman was the medical professional in town, and Monte knew that the aid station would be closed, so he took Nancy directly to Coach Wellman's home, so his wife, the new practitioner in town, could look after her. Fortunately, Nancy was more scared than anything else. Although she had a few bruises and one small abrasion, her injuries were relatively minor. While Janice attended to Nancy, Coach Wellman called the police. Within a few minutes, there was the bulky and arrogant Constable McMillan.

Not even courteous enough to ask Nancy how she was, he immediately blurted out his usual insult when dealing with teenagers. "So, your nefarious activities have finally caught up with you, Nancy."

Janice Wellman was shocked at the treatment her patient was receiving from the inhospitable Constable McMillan. She immediately stood up and glared disrespectfully at him and said in a direct and highly irreverent tone, "this young lady has just gone through a traumatic experience, Constable. I would expect you could be a little more sympathetic, and as a public servant, try to apprehend whoever did this to her."

"You haven't been in this town long enough to understand that this girl," and then he turned and pointed directly at Monte, "and this boy here, too, has been nothing but trouble for the police department for years. I

79

wouldn't be surprised if he wasn't the one who did this to her. I know they had a heated verbal argument this summer, and in spite of the fact they both think they are some type of hockey heroes now, they are still nothing but a couple of juvenile delinquents to me."

As the Constable let lose with his verbal barrage, Coach Wellman, who was sitting in a chair, holding the now sleeping daughter of Nancy Running Elk, eased up, placed the child on the sofa and moved toward McMillan. Wellman, about 188 centimetres (6:2) and 95 kilos (210 pounds) was not an imposing figure physically, but he had always been a man who stood tall against the arrogance of those with power and wealth. In Constable McMillan, he saw a man who abused his power, and obviously thought his position was supposed to make people fear and respect him. Wellman felt neither fear nor respect for a man who was obviously prejudiced against Aboriginals. Not wanting to cause an argument, he was calm, but stern. "I assume you are going to take the young lady's statement and do something about arresting her assailant."

McMillan replied, "sure, I'll take her statement, but I cannot vouch that it will be the truth."

Nancy and Monte both stood stoically silent, because they had learned that since McMillan had come to town nearly three years ago, the police had never been too concerned about violence perpetrated against the Aboriginals, who made up about 80% of the town's population, since it was adjacent to the Cree Reserve. They had learned to expect little in help from a man who looked with disdain on them, and they did fear him.

Then, Nancy and Monte heard something from the coach that made them realize more than ever that he was a man who was willing to put himself on the line for those who suffered injustice. "Listen McMillan, you are a public servant. I, my wife, the child sleeping on the sofa and these two young people are the public, and we expect our public servants to do what they are supposed to do – serve us in our time of need. You can serve us, or I will call your bosses in Regina and get them to send someone up here who will serve us. We pay your salary, so you work for us. We don't work for you. Take the girl's statement, get off your butt and do something about this heinous assault. Your personal opinion about these two people is immaterial, just like my opinion of you is irrelevant, because if you knew what my opinion of you was, you'd probably arrest me. Are you going to do your job or not."

McMillan, was not only surprised by Wellman's defence of the two young people, but incredibly taken aback by his refusal to cower in fear before the law. Deciding that discretion was the better part of valour, he turned to Nancy and said, "so, who was it did this to you?"

Nancy, surprised that McMillan was actually being somewhat respectful, decided to tell him exactly what happened. "Constable, I really didn't see the assailant. I was walking with Jasmine down Watson Road, near where the old tavern was. I saw something moving in the bushes beside the road, and thought maybe it was an animal stalking us. We got to the bend in the road, and I went to the right. He had on a white hood covering his face and a dark jacket. That is when he jumped out of the bushes and grabbed me. I let go of Jasmine's hand and started pounding him on his chest. He had the hardest chest. It was like I was hitting a rock. My hands hurt so bad."

As Nancy told the story of the assault, Monte felt indignation swelling up inside him. She was a tough girl. She proved that every time she skated onto the ice. The boys on the opposing teams made it a point to go after her, but she never backed down. No doubt, she stood her ground against her assailant, but Monte wished he had been there to help her and little Jasmine. He looked at her standing there, glanced over at her sleeping daughter, and an incredible desire to protect her and the child overwhelmed him. At that moment, she wasn't just a tough hockey player, she was a vulnerable, fragile young lady Monte wanted to protect from harm.

McMillan adjusted his bullet proof vest as Nancy continued her story. "Well, my hand hurt so bad that I had to stop hitting him. I collapsed to the ground and he said something that sent a chill through me."

McMillan, his disinterest seemingly totally subsided now, asked, "and what was it he said."

"He said that I was finished in this town and needed to get out of here immediately, or I would gravely suffer the consequences. He disguised his voice, because he talked with a huskiness that was obviously an attempt to camouflage the way he really sounded. Consequently, I think I must know him, but I haven't a clue as to who he was."

McMillan felt that even though he had no real interest in what happened to a young woman he considered a miscreant, he would go through the motions of an investigation to satisfy Coach Wellman and his wife, so that they would assume he was doing his duty. Yet, deep inside he felt he had no duty when it came to Aboriginals.

McMillan asked Nancy to accompany him back to the scene of the assault, but Janice Wellman insisted that would have to wait until the morning, as she would not release the traumatized young girl from her charge until then.

Reluctantly, McMillan agreed and left. Meanwhile, Janice instructed the coach and Monte to take Jasmine to her grandmother and explain what had happened to Nancy. She would keep an eye on Nancy until the morning, when she would accompany her to see Constable McMillan.

Fortunately, Monte was a lad equal to any occasion. Of course, he had never had an experience like this before; but somehow he seemed to understand that the first, indeed, only thing to be done at the moment, was to get Jaasmine safely back home, and leave Nancy to the care of capable Janice Wellman. He felt fortunate that he and Nancy had found two good friends in the coach and his wife, who were allies against indifference, prejudice and injustice in a town that for far too long had turned a blind eye to it. For some reason that he couldn't understand, he was feeling like things were about to change for the good.

Walking with Monte to Nancy's home, the coach kept offering to carry little Jasmine for awhile, but Monte said she wasn't heavy, not to worry about it. Coach noticed how lovingly Monte seemed to hold her. This was the boy who so many felt was a rogue, but coach saw through the façade of misconceptions. This was a boy who had a soft and loving heart. He also began to understand that it might be more than the mere fact that he was looking after a little girl. It was Nancy's little girl, and that made her special to Monte. Maybe Monte didn't realize that he was enamoured with Nancy, but the wise old coach had, himself, had many romantic interludes over the years, and he could see the budding love developing in Monte. He wondered if Nancy felt the same way.

The next morning Janice Wellman went down to see Constable McMillan with Nancy. Out at the crime scene, Janice noticed that McMillan's animosity toward Nancy had returned, as he seemed curt and antagonistic over every detail about the assault. Apparently, he had decided that the lack of a physical description made it next to impossible to find the culprit.

Nancy went off to school, and Janice Wellman went on with her duties back at the aid station. Yet, both of them would spend the day laboriously reflecting on the events that had brought them together. Due to Constable McMillan's irritating and biased actions, Janice felt a keen awareness now of the undercurrent of prejudice against the native population in Cree Lake. As an Aboriginal herself, she had often experienced subtle discrimination from people who didn't even know that their subconscious prejudice was being manifested in the ways they acted when around Aboriginals. Many times she had noticed shop keepers keep a wary eye on her when she would wander through a store, obviously assuming she was more likely to engage in theft than the white customers. And how many times had she been treated discourteously by people simply because she was an Aboriginal? She recalled the time when, with her husband, she was standing in line at a convenience store. Two Aboriginals were in front of them in line, but because her husband was white, the clerk motioned for him to come to the front of the line. Typical of her husband, he threw the things he had down on the counter and said, "keep your merchandise, I would never buy anything from a prejudice jerk like you."

Her husband, although not Aboriginal, had helped her to find her own roots. He had taught her to appreciate who she was and to take pride in being a member of a noble race. In fact, that was why she was in Cree Lake. She gave up a somewhat privileged existence to administer medical aid to people who were cut-off from so-called modern civilization. She felt a strong kinship with the marginalized in a world where all the material wealth only flowed to those at the top. She had come to Canada as an escape from what she saw as a banal existence in a place where abject poverty was allowed to flourish alongside opulent affluence, and there seemed to be none who were willing to right this affront to common decency in a world where greed was proclaimed a virtue, rather than an immoral impediment to the progress of the human race.

Janice's husband had dutifully followed her, because, as a moderately successful writer, he said he could live anywhere she wanted to sit up practice. They had turned their backs on the urban jungles of concrete and steel, for what they hoped would be a more peaceful and tranquil life. Yet, in the midst of the tranquility the two sought, they now found that perverse prejudice and judgmental arrogance was not just exclusive to the city. Additionally, there was something mysterious and sinister going on in Cree Lake

Despite all the turmoil over the robbery and assault, Friday night had come, and the game at the lake against Regina was about to begin. Monte was ready to play, and Nancy had sufficiently recovered from her injuries to suit up for what would likely be a hard fought game. Yet, what happened was actually unexpected. With the stands overflowing with fans, the entire lakeside was filled with eager onlookers sitting in folding chairs as word of just how good this team had become was rapidly spreading.

Since the team was made up entirely of First Nations youth, it was surprising to see the large number of non-Aboriginals who were part of the crowd. Was this team a catalyst that would unite an often racially divided town? Coach Wellman had been well-known for his penchant as a promoter in his sojourns as a coach in other places, but in reality, he had done very little to promote this team, other than encourage his players to realize that they were more than just players, they were entertainers. As such, they owed it to those willing to pay the $3 admission to provide them with entertaining play.

The experienced coach, the Cree Lake team and the crowd were somewhat in awe when they saw the tough-looking Regina team skate onto the ice with obviously shiny new uniforms and a military like precession that almost made you want to gasp at their professional, methodical-like demeanour. These guys were a determined bunch of players who seemed to exude a confident nature.

Coach Wellman called over his charges and they huddled around the bench. He could see that they were all in a state of dread as the mere size of the Regina team they were about to face had intimidated them. In a calm, resolute tone of voice, he prepared them for battle. "Those guys are big. They are the cream of the crop from a city with nearly 200,000 people from which to select the very best players available. Do not be intimated by their physical size. As a child, I was often told a tale of a small boy named David who slew an imposing giant named Goliath with a tiny sling shot. It may be a fairy tale. I do not know for sure. Yet, I do know that I have coached many teams with much less talent than this team has, and they slew giants time and time again, because they realized that a person's size has nothing to do with the size of their heart. Go get 'um."

What followed surprised not only the fans, the Regina team and the coaches, but it even shocked the Cree Lake team itself. Before they realized it, these giant slayers were in front 4-0 in the first period. Destroying the imposing Regina team under the leadership of Nancy Running Elk, who scored 4 goals and had 5 assists, in a 11-0 shellacking of Regina, the following night they defeated the same team 7-0. The word would be out all over the province, there was a team in Cree Lake to be reckoned with.

After the last game, a jubilant Coach Wellman had great praise for a team that had jelled like a few others he had coached to championships over the years. "You are doing splendid work, fellows," he told them, with a look of pride on his face, "and the way you played this weekend was worthy of any team I have ever coached. And the team you played fought tooth and nail to hold you back. They did not give you these victories in an easy fashion. You simply out-smarted and out-played them. Not a single one of you played an individual game. You all played a team game. You are now all aware that we win or lose together. There is no *I* on this team, only *we*. The pride I have in being called coach by you; I will never be able to put into words. Thank you for giving me the honour of sharing this weekend of glory with you."

It can be easily understood why Monte, Ted and Nancy were feeling in particularly good humour, as they walked to town after the game, with little Jasmine in tow after her grandmother left and went home, having exhausted herself wildly cheering for her beloved granddaughter in whom she had so much pride and hope, in spite of the fact she had gotten pregnant at the tender age of 14, and often been in trouble with authorities. Nancy's grandmother was a beacon of light in the darkness for both Nancy and Jasmine.

"I haven't had a fair chance to say a word to you two about what happened to Nancy," Ted unceremoniously broke in, "and I am incredibly anxious to hear what really happened, rather than get it from second and third hand sources like I usually get most of my information. That is if you want to share it with me, Nancy."

"Nancy, holding Jasmine's hand as they strolled through the downtown park, said somewhat morosely, "I don't really have that much to say, Ted. All I know is that I went with Jasmine Monday night, like I always do, to the Wilton's place. We stayed about two hours, and on the way back I seemed to sense that there was something or somebody following us in the bushes by the side of the road. Suddenly, when I got to the bend, I was simply furiously attacked and told by a hoarse voice to get out of town while I still could. I am surprised I could handle the puck so well with my stick this weekend, because my grip wasn't as tight as usual, since my hands still ache from pounding the person on his hard chest. That is it. That is all I know, and all I will probably ever know, because we all three know that McMillan doesn't care about what happened to me. If I had been killed, he would probably have been pleased."

Monte, not one to defend Constable McMillan, did however offer a somewhat defensive comment, "well, McMillan is pretty sinister and conniving, but I really don't think he is the type person to celebrate a murder. I don't have much respect for him Nancy, but if you had been murdered, I do think he would have been a bit more proactive."

Nancy, at the mention of the term murder seemed to go into deep contemplative thought and her eyes even became misty. Monte wondered why she was suddenly so sensitive and pensive. Then, she made a puzzling comment: "you know, murder is not always murder. Sometimes what seems to be murder is actually an act to shield someone from harm."

Both boys were confused by the statement, but had no time to explore it with her, because Jasmine was wildly chasing a squirrel, and Nancy had to grab her in order to prevent her from running into the street. As Nancy took Jasmine by the hand and scolded her, Monte said, "hey, how about a soda at the general store. I got a few dollars, and I bet Jasmine would like a soda."

Ted nodded his head in the negative, sensing that what Monte really wanted was to be alone with Nancy, and said, "gotta go home, buddy. Maybe another time. See you guys at school Monday."

Waving goodbye to Ted, Nancy held Jasmine's right hand with her left hand as they crossed the street. Little Jasmine reached up and instinctively took Monte's right hand. Monte suddenly wondered what it would be like to hold Nancy's hand. He thought back on how light Nancy felt when he carried her to Coach Wellman's house. Even in her heavy winter coat, he could sense her softness that night. Hey, what was wrong with him?

Nancy looked over at Monte and smiled. She knew things, dark and mysterious things, that she felt she could never tell him, but still she sensed that Monte was becoming more than just a team-mate and friend.

Ironically, at the same time, Monte was thinking about her mentioning going to the Wilton's on Mondays. He still did not have the courage to come out and ask her why she was always there on Monday evenings? There had to be a good reason for it. Yet, he did not want to risk their friendship by appearing to be overly inquisitive about something that, in reality, was most definitely none of his business.

The next day at school, the players from the team were all swamped with affection from adoring chums who were taking great pride in the accomplishments of the team that had been together for so long and been a town pariah until the current season. Suddenly, they were looked upon as something which the backwater town, isolated from the rest of the province, could take enormous pride in as newspapers all over the province were beginning to pick up the story of the "little town and reserve that could."

As they left school that day, Ted asked Monte how things went with Nancy. Monte seemed to take offence to the question. "What do you mean, how did things go? We are just friends. We had a soda, and I walked her and Jasmine home – end of story."

"O.K. O.K. Don't get touchy. I was just asking a question. You see, I am interested in Nancy's welfare. I'm beginning to feel sorry for saying some of the mean things I did about her. It must be terribly hard for a girl who's always been termed bad to get people to see her good side. Nancy is a known commodity in this town, and people point their fingers at her with scorn, and talk openly about her getting pregnant at 14. There are constantly rumours about who the father might be. Meanwhile, most people say Nancy is so promiscuous only a blood test of the whole male population of Cree Lake, maybe the entire province, could really reveal who the father is."

That really set off a tirade of indignation from Monte. "Listen, it is nobody's business but Nancy's. Also, name one male you know in this town who has ever really been out with Nancy, other than Lenny. Supposedly, Lenny was her boyfriend long after her pregnancy, but I have never seen any proof whatsoever of a romantic relationship between them."

Ted was not really surprised by his friend's defence of Nancy, as he, too, had become eager to defend her against nefarious charges. "Hey buddy, I am not attacking her. I have grown to respect and admire her. I am just curious, that's all. And I know you are curious, too."

Monte was a bit calmer now. "Yeah, I admit I am curious, but I don't think it is anybody's business. I have actually been thinking about following her out to the Wilton's to see what goes on out there on Monday evenings, but I just can't bring myself to do it. Nancy is my friend now, and I should respect her privacy."

"I guess you are right, but I sure would like to know what their connection is. I know about the alibi thing, but

I just don't understand why she feels the need to go out there once a week."

Just then, Coach Wellman pulled alongside them and said, "hop in boys and I'll give you a lift to town. I've decided to post bail for Lenny Dan. I think it is a shame that boy has been locked up all this time just because of a vendetta against him by Constable McMillan. Guilty or not, he deserves to be out until his trial. I have always said the rich get a fine and the poor get jail. That boy deserves to be treated fairly. Anyway, I'm going to see his mother and if she agrees, I will post the bond for her."

The boys enthusiastically hopped into coach's car. They stopped at the Dan farm and Lenny's mother answered the door after several knocks. She looked frightened at seeing the coach and the two boys there on the porch. A paleness seemed to ascend over her, but no sooner had the coach spoken in his kindly fashion than the anxious expression fled from her pale face.

"Please excuse me for dropping in on you, Mrs. Dan," said the coach, after they had been ushered into the humble sitting-room, where a wood-fire burned on the hearth, "but I just couldn't stand it any longer. I want to stand bail for your boy, so you can have him home again with you till his trial date is set. I only ask that you sign a promissory note to me in the amount of $1000. Obviously, once he shows up for trial and I have my bail money back, I will tear up the promissory note."

Lenny's mother looked embarrassed. She twisted her apron in her nervous fingers, and seemed very near the point of tears. "Oh! it's kind of you, Mr. Wellman, indeed it is!" she finally exclaimed, as she looked up at the smiling, sympathetic big man, "he does swear to me that he is innocent, but I can't figure out why all that stuff was hidden in the barn. How could it have gotten there?"

Coach replied, "Mrs. Dan, I am not judging the boy's guilt or innocence. I just think it is unfair for someone who is poor to sit in jail while those with means are allowed the privilege of posting bail. That is not right. I detest a world where the poor are put upon continuously while the well-off and well-connected get a free pass. Your son may not be perfect, but neither are a lot of other boys who get the privilege of bail because their parents can afford it. I just want a little bit of justice in a world where it is in short supply."

Mrs. Dan looked astonished, as Monte and Ted nodded their heads in a agreement with what the coach had said. Here was a man who understood the plight of those who lived a marginalized existence in a world where everything seemed to favour those who deserved it least. Coach was one man who saw suffering and tried to heal it.

Signing a promissory note, Mrs. Dan thanked the coach. He assured her that he would have her son home within the next few hours.

"Thank you again and again for your kindness to a poor woman and a mother, sir!" she exclaimed with a half-suppressed sob in her voice as they left the humble abode, "but there does not seem to be any doubt about my boy's guilt, much as I hate to acknowledge it. His association with Tipper Running Bear may be his problem, because I know Constable McMillan has it in for him. Even Nancy Running Elk hung around with him, and she isn't a favourite of Constable McMillan either. Although, I must say that girl seemed to always try to get my boy to do right. Many a time she said to me that she would try to look after him. She is a real good girl, no matter what everybody else says about her."

Once outside, the boys shook hands with the big man. Monte and Ted were feeling more drawn towards him than ever.

"We'll see you at practice tomorrow coach, " said the boys as they decided to walk the short distance to their homes.

"Yes, boys," the coach replied, "I hope the team doesn't get too cocky after our victories over Regina. North Battleford will be no push-over, and on their home ice, we will have to play really well to come out on top."

As the Coach pulled out into the road, Ted and Monte ambled toward their homes and they noticed the front end of a police cruiser partially sticking out from behind Mrs. Dan's barn. Was it McMillan, and if so, why was he there?

Fearful of getting into trouble, the boys ignored what they saw. They continued down the road, and glanced over their shoulders and saw the police car pull out and slowly move down the road far behind the coach's car. Looking at the car from the back, it was easy to recognize the head of Constable McMillan. There was also bald-headed man in the car with him. Why had they been at the Dan farm? Why were they following Coach Wellman?

CHAPTER 10
UNTIL YOU HAVE WALKED IN THEIR SHOES

Coach Wellman walked into the police station and told the clerk he had $1000 in cash to post as bail for Lenny Dan. The clerk said that he did not have the authority to release him.

The coach was a bit direct when he said, "you don't need authority. His bail has been set. You are the clerk. I have the bail. Take the money, give me a receipt and release the man."

Just at that point, Constable McMillan walked in, accompanied by the owner of the general store and cafe, Harold Lasky, who, was for some reason, furiously scratching his bald head. The constable was not particularly pleased to see the coach. "Hey, coach, you need to stick to coaching hockey and leave the social work to the experts."

The coach, never one to suffer quietly the arrogance of those who thought their position of authority made them more exalted than the average person, was blunt and curt in replying. "I'm not doing social work. I am simply looking for some fairness in a justice system that expects those with no wealth, no position or the right skin colour to sit serenely in the slammer while those with some juice receive preferential treatment. Let the young man out, or I will have a Human Rights Commission lawyer up here tomorrow, along with the media and anybody else I can interest in seeing how you are administering justice like a backwater tyrant with no respect for the people you are supposed to serve. Instruct your clerk here to take my money, and I definitely want a receipt."

Constable McMillan did not say anything to the coach. He just looked at the clerk, nodded affirmatively, turned and signalled for Harold Lasky to follow him into his office. They closed the class door behind them. The clerk took Coach Wellman's money, wrote a receipt and got up to get Lenny Dan.

While waiting, the coach, through the class door of McMillan's office, noticed Lasky pull his chair up close to McMillan and lean forward as if whispering something highly secretive. Then, Lenny came out with a look of surprise on his face.

Smiling, coach said, "let's get you home to your mom Lenny."

Lenny, still in shock that he had been released said, "you bailing me out coach?"

"Well, I put the money up, but your mom signed a promissory note, so I'd say your mom is the one bailing you out, not me. I hope you won't make a fool out of her."

For someone who was supposed to be tough, Lenny seemed awfully sedate and serene. "I won't make her regret it. I didn't do it coach. I know it looks bad for me, but I was set-up by somebody – set up good."

Coach Wellman put his right arm around Lenny's shoulder and said, "you need to get a lawyer to talk to about that, son. I'll help you and your mom find one."

To Wellman and Lenny's surprise, standing outside the lockup was Ted and Monte. Monte, whispered softly, "coach, Ted and I have something we need to tell you. It's important we think."

"Sure, get in the car boys, you can ride with me to take Lenny home."

Acknowledging Lenny with an afformative nod of their heads, Monte and Ted climbed in the backseat and Lenny got in the front alongside coach. For a reason he couldn't fathom, because he had never liked Lenny, Monte placed his hand on his shoulder and said, "glad to see you out, Lenny."

Ted, equal in his disdain for Lenny, was surprised when he, himself, added to what Monte said. "Yeah, me too man."

Perhaps, the kindness of the two was why Lenny brought up Nancy Running Elk, since he knew the two boys and the coach were interested in her welfare. It was not particularly the conversation that the coach wanted to have, but Lenny was intent on letting him know something about Nancy.

"Nancy is a heck of a hockey player, coach. I have watched her play for years, but until you encouraged her, she never really figured that they would let her play on the boys team. You really deserve credit for giving her and Myrna a chance. Those girls are something else. You two also Monte and Ted. You have been really nice to both of those girls. Nancy really respects both of you. She is lucky to have you all as friends."

Coach Wellman, surprised at Lenny's kindness, simply nodded his head in agreement. Then Lenny dropped a bombshell. "Hey, Tipper and I were really going to rob the store. In fact, we even tried to get Nancy to help us. We wanted her to drive the van. She would have none of it. Yet, she was too loyal to rat us out. That is why she went down to the Wilton's on that Saturday night. She knew she would need an alibi. Turned out she did. Of course, with McMillan out to get you, it doesn't make much difference whether you have an alibi or not."

Coach Wellman, surprised, but delighted at Lenny's candour, decided to see if he could get some more information out of him. "So, you are telling us that you did rob the store?"

"No, that's just it. We were in the store when we heard Mr. Lasky telling McMillan he had over $50,000 worth of cigarettes coming in that Friday, and that he would be distributing some of them to other stores in Northern Saskatchewan, and he also had $30,000 worth of hunting rifles coming in. So, we figured it was our opportunity get our hands on the merchandise, blow this place and unload the haul down in Regina and never come back."

Wellman was fascinated by what he was hearing, and listened intently as Lenny continued. "Anyway, we are set to rob the place at 11:00 PM, when we park the van out on Comstock Road and walk into town to case the joint and make sure the coast is clear before bringing the van in.

Coach interrupted Lenny. "Didn't you think eleven o'clock was a little risky? People might still be up."

"Coach, Tipper and I aren't the ripest apples on the tree. Every single time we have done something illegal, we've got caught. You'd think that we would figure out that we weren't cut out to be thieves. To show you how dumb we are, even when we plan a robbery but don't commit it, we get blamed for it."

Chuckling a bit, Monte offered some solace about stupidity to Lenny. "Hey man, Ted and I know something about being dumb. You've got nothing on us. We've had our share of run-ins with McMillan, and we always come out on the short end of the stick.

Wellman, fascinated by the story said, "you are telling me that there was a robbery that night, you two planned it, but when you arrrived, there were two other people robbing the place."

"You got it, coach. We notice that there's a blue SUV parked in the back of the store and two people with hoodies pulled over their heads loading it with cartoons of cigarettes and rifles. We stayed in the bushes and observed them. We didn't recognize them. They never said a word to each other until the shortest one kind of laughed and said over the top of the car as they were getting ready to leave, *let's take it to the bank, man.*"

Wellman, always prided himself on being a bit of an amateur detective, as when he was young, he loved to watch movies and TV shows about private detectives. When his mother wasn't around, he would even read the racy Mickey Spillane novels about Mike Hammer, Private Eye. In fact, he used to fantasize about getting involved in mystery and intrigue. Of course, there was always a femme fatale in the story, and good old Coach Wellman would eventually wind up with her in his arms – in his dreams at least.

As they pulled in front of Lenny's home, coach said, "Lenny, I believe you didn't commit the robbery, and I will do all I can to see that you get justice. Meanwhile, go in and get some rest – and also comfort you mother a bit."

Lenny, not acting at all like the miscreant he was made out to be, was gracious. "Thanks so much coach," then he looked at Monte and Ted and continued, "thanks to you two, also. It is nice to know there are a few people who have some sympathy for you. Good luck against Melfort tomorrow night. I'll be there cheering for you."

Ted, Monte and the coach were pretty quiet on the way back, but they were all thinking the same thing. Who actually robbed the store? Why was McMillan so intent on railroading Lenny, Tipper and Nancy for the crime? They were also thinking about how they may have also misjudged Lenny. Maybe he wasn't that bad after all. O.K., so he planned to rob the store. Maybe that was bad, but how many banks robbed people of their homes every day without anyone going to jail? How many business people on Bay Street or Wall Street stole people's life savings every day with complete impunity? Finally, in regards to Lenny, they all considered that old adage: *you can never understand a person until you have walked in their shoes.*

CHAPTER 11
SOMETHING MORE EXPLOSIVE
WAS ABOUT TO OCCUR

Like most events, the robbery became old news, except the day when Tipper was finally arrested by McMillan and charged with the robbery. It seems that the Chesterfield cigarette discarded by Tipper and picked up by Grif was the key link connecting Tipper to the nefarious deed, although, none of the loot had been recovered, other than what was found at Lenny's place. The cigarette itself was a key piece of evidence, since that brand was new to the store and had, at the time, not been sold over the counter. It certainly appeared the boys were going to be convicted.

Unlike Lenny, Tipper was able to post bail immediately. Meanwhile, Lenny and Tipper were offered the services of an attorney out of Prince Albert, thanks to the coach, who went to the legal aid society for help. Because of his case load, the attorney kept getting the trial put off.

As the months passed, the Cree Lake Badgers continued to mystify the town, as they were still undefeated. Their defence had become tenacious, and the play of Nancy, Myrna and Monte had galvanized the team into a belief that they were nothing short of invincible. Furthermore, the goal tending tandem of Jake Thundercloud and Bobby Joel seemed to have placed a veritable brick wall in front of the net. They were working on a string of five straight shut-outs.

By the end of February, they were 34-0, with only a two game series at home against Prince Albert standing between them and an undefeated season that would put them as the top seed in the Northern Saskatchewan district play-offs. The games were so popular that the town had increased seating capacity at the rink to 400.

As time progressed, the entire team began to coalesce around the leadership of the two female players. Being a team made up of adolescent boys, one might expect that the boys were enamoured with the attractive young ladies. Yet, it appeared most of the boys were simply accepting them as team-mates rather than romantic paramours.

Myrna did find herself drawn to the cavalier-acting Ted, and they became somewhat of an item around town. Nancy, on the other hand, was known to be constantly turning down pleas from some team-mates for dates, as she said that her spare time was for studying, otherwise coach would toss her off the team for bad grades, or for spending time with her daughter, who was seeing less and less of her since she got involved with hockey and was more devoted to her studies.

Then, there was Monte. Although he, Nancy and little Jasmine were often together about town, Monte sensed no romantic interest in him whatsoever from Nancy. Yet, for months, those images of her continued to dance in his head, even while he spent time with other girls. Still, he kept telling himself that they were just friends. The fact that she was the first thing on his mind every morning and the last thing on his mind every night was mere coincidence.

The day of the game, the town was abuzz with activity in preparation for a weekend that was like none the little village of Cree Lake had ever seen before. A TV crew was even flown in from a TV station in Regina to do a story on the little town of Cree Lake and its First Nations hockey team that was attracting so much attention. When the talent-laden Prince Albert team arrived in a convoy of snowmobiles from the road where their bus had dropped them off, they were surprised to see all the attention the game was getting from the media and the local townsfolk. They had heard of the success the team was having, but they were confident of victory, as they had only lost two games themselves, both to a Saskatoon team that was not undefeated, but had played much tougher competition than Cree Lake. The players all felt that Cree Lake was about to see an end to its winning streak.

The game was scheduled for 7:00 PM that night, and the lights had been turned on at 4:30 PM, since darkness comes extremely early that far north. The fans started lining up as early as 4:00 PM so eager they were to get a good seat. By 5:00 PM the regular stands were filled and by 5:30 PM, so were the temporary seats set up behind the goal on the shoreline side. By 6:00 PM, fans were lining the banks and climbing on tops of cars parked along the shoreline. Constable McMillan and his boys stopped fans from going on the far lakeside to sit for fear that the weight of the crowd might cause the ice to start cracking. It appeared the whole village had showed up for the game.

Although many teams complained about the bitter cold and the intensity of the whipping wind blowing over the frozen lake, this night there was no wind, the temperature was only slightly below freezing and the northern lights were not illuminating as brightly as normal. In fact, grey clouds hung angularly in the sky above the rink. There was a surreal feel about that night, as if something sinister might be lurking just below the surface of this quaint little village. The Cree Lake team looked out from their warming hut at the grey sky, and Coach Wellman could see that there was a tension there that had not existed before that night. Was his team finally experiencing trepidation?

Coach Wellman was never one to over-practice a team, or, for that matter, one to overly motivate a team with verbal and psychological ploys. After all, each player knew what he or she had to do, and if prepared mentally and physically, they should be ready to do their jobs. It was not always about talent. It often simply came down to execution and positioning, so the opponent was kept off balance and confused. The coach knew he did not have the most talented team in Saskatchewan, but he genuinely felt they were the most determined and motivated bunch of players he ever had the privilege to coach.

When they skated onto the ice for warm-ups, Wellman noticed a tightness in their strides when they saw the huge throng that had turned out to support what was once termed a team of rogues who would rather win a fight on the ice than win a game. That had changed. The team rarely took a bad penalty, as the coach had admonished them for foolishness, and reminded them that tough, physical play did not have to include unnecessary roughness, penalties or fights. They had come together as a team, and their unselfishness made them a force to be reckoned with on the icy surface of honour. Yet, Coach Wellman sensed an uneasiness that night. It was there, just beneath the surface.

Lining up for the initial face-off, the normally supremely confident and stoic Nancy seemed incredibly diminutive surrounded by the towering hulks of the Prince Albert team. Her grip on the stick seemed less impervious than usual. She was scared. And Monte, on her left wing, seemed to glide gently back from his opponent, apparently in deference to his immense size.

Myrna, on the right wing, did not do her usual stare-down with her opponent. The defensemen stood flat-footed, seemingly disinterested.

Coach was about to call them to the bench and put out another line, but just then, the puck was dropped. Prince Albert roared across the Cree Lake blue line and the defensemen were left glaring at the speed of the Prince Albert forwards. Wham, bam, slam – back of the net. 1-0 Prince Albert with only 7 seconds elapsed.

Coach Wellman immediately replaced the line. The line brought off sat on the bench dejected with looks of disgust on their faces. The coach bent down and said, "shake it off. You guys have the jitters. You are better than this."

Within a minute, Prince Albert had scored another goal. Score 2-0, and Wellman decides to go back to his first line. They lose the face-off, and Nancy is levelled viciously by a check from behind that is ignored by the referee. As she lies on the ice writhing in pain, Prince Albert drives another goal home at the 5 minute mark. 3-0, and things look bleak when Monte and Myrna are both assessed roughing penalties for going after the guy who hit Nancy. As Nancy is escorted to the warming hut for Janice Wellman to assess, the team seems as if they are coming apart as they struggle with a 5 on 3 power play. Prince Albert scores a goal at 5:35 and it is 4-0. Getting one player back from the penalty box, Coach Wellman sees that the team is in a desperate situation. What can he do? While he is mentally reviewing his options, Prince Albert scores at the seven minute mark, 5-0.

The coach thought it unfair to make Jake Thundercloud suffer any longer. He pulled the goalie and inserted his back-up, who, though not great, was still adequate at stopping the puck if only he had a decent defence in front of him, which unfortunately was non-existent at the time.

Sensing that all might be lost, the coach called his one time-out. Several team members, Monte being the most vocal, were voicing concern about Nancy. Coach Wellman sent Jake Thundercloud to the warming hut to check on her. "Listen, all I am asking you to do is hold on for the rest of the period. Don't give these guys any more goals. We can still win this game. We are that good, but we can't win it if you don't stop them and stop them now. I don't want any more pucks in our net. Just get through this period and we will regroup and give these guys a fight. Got it."

Jake came back to the bench just as the referee signalled the end of the time out. "She is fine, Mrs. Wellman is putting a compress on her back, and she'll be on the ice by the second period."

Their spirits lifted with news of Nancy's impending return, they skated brilliantly the rest of the period, holding off wave after wave of their swift skating opponents who seemed a bit shocked that they were now unable to score. Backup goalie, Bobby Joel, was making some incredible stops, and the fans, who had been dismayed by what happened the first few minutes were urging the team on, hoping that they could somehow get back in the game. Even with the return of Nancy for the second period, it seemed the Badgers just couldn't find the back of the net. Still behind 5-0 after the second period, a few grumbling fans remarked that it was now all over, the undefeated season was no longer possible. Meanwhile, as the Zamboni made ice, Coach Wellman, in the warming hut with a dejected team, asked himself how he could arouse these fine young people and at least get them to make an effort for one more period, win or lose. He had been in dire situations before with no hope, and this was one of the most hopeless situations he had ever encountered as a coach. He knew they were defeated, but he also knew that it was not always the fact that you lost, but how you lost that counted. He wanted these guys to go down fighting, so they could continue to hold their heads high.

He called Bobby Joel over to a corner of the hut, put his arm around him and said, "Bobby, you have been remarkable, but Jake's confidence has been broken. I won't do it without your O.K., because you have stopped everything that has come your way, but if you will say you approve, I want to put Jake back in. What do you say."

"I say you are the coach, and if that is what you think should be done, then I am all for it."

Smiling, pulling his charge close and patting him on the back, the coach said nothing, but Bobby knew that he had won the respect of the man he admired. That, in itself, was more valuable than playing in goal the last period.

What follows is not the exact speech given by Coach Wellman, as there is no recording of it, but the speech has been oft paraphrased by the young men and women who were there when it was made, so it is fairly accurate.

"Gentlemen and ladies, I have coached many teams over the years, but I have never enjoyed any team as much as I have enjoyed this one. You may think I say that to all my teams, and in all fairness, I have said it to other teams, but when I was saying it, for that time it was true.

This time it is true of this team. I suppose the reason I enjoy coaching this team so much is that you are a group of people, who like me, think that the world is a very unfair and unreasonable place, and you refuse to accept the injustice all about you. That is why the term rogues was often used to describe you. I was told you were un-coachable, because you didn't like to follow orders. What they really meant was that you refused to march in lock-step with your peers who see injustice and do not stand against it.

"Well, in Germany during World War II, a lot of people also followed orders. That is the excuse used by those who oversaw the gas chambers. A few years ago, in the nation south of us, people listened to incredible lies about weapons of mass destruction and went along with an illegal war and the torture of soldiers as young as 15 years old. That 15 year old was a Canadian citizen, and the government of this country stood idly by while this was occurring, because they were fearful and timid about offending a neighbour that was more powerful than this country is. Thus, they refused to stand against injustice, simply because they feared the power of those who practiced the injustices."

"I admire each and everyone of you, because you have the courage to stand up to authority. It is not enough for you to be told to do something. You ask why? If the Germans who watched the Jews being carted off to concentration camps had asked why, there would not have been a Holocaust. If the citizens south of us had asked why, 4500 soldiers would not have lost their lives in a needless war for the oil riches of Iraq. If they had asked why, countless others would have not been cruelly tortured at the behest of evil leaders who thought they were above the law."

108

"You might be asking yourselves, what the hell does this have to do with a hockey game? The answer is that it is at the very centre of what this game is all about. We are a team, and we stand together against adversity,"

The coach paused, walked over to Nancy and Myrna. He placed his hand first on the shoulder of Nancy, then Myrna. He turned and continued.

"These young ladies have endured abuse all year, because the boys on the other teams resent them being on the ice. They are supposed to play with girls, because they are not good enough to compete with boys. Even some of you thought that yourselves at the beginning of the season, but today, you all know they belong on this team. We have succeeded because all of you have never once hesitated to stand with these young ladies against the abuse they suffer. There is not a single one of you who will not stand with your team-mates no matter how tough the odds. We are now facing overwhelming odds against winning this game. I am not here to tell you that we will win this game. In fact, the odds are against it, but I am here to tell you this. When Jake Thundercloud leads you out for the third period and proudly stands in net ready to do battle, each and everyone of you will give your maximum effort so that our opponents will know that they have faced a team that will not go meekly into that gentle night. We shall rage against the storm. We will fight with our last breath."

"You have hundreds of fans out there who are disappointed, but they will not be disappointed in you as long as they know you gave everything you had out there on the rink, regardless of the final score. This year, you have all proved that you do not have to come from a big place to do big things. There is no shame in losing as long

as you go down fighting. You have to kick as long as you have a foot. You have to punch as long as you have a fist. You have to bite as long as you have teeth. And when you are footless, fist-less and toothless, you can use whatever is left to fight against all odds."

Nancy stood up defiantly and shouted, "let's go get 'um guys."

There were fewer fans in the stands, as many were so disillusioned with what had happened that they simply figured they might as well avoid the inevitable. Yet, later, even those who were not there to see what happened, somehow mysteriously would say they stayed until the very end. In fact, even those who stayed at home that night were actually at the game, as no one wanted to admit they had missed what occurred on that frozen lake one Friday night.

Within the first minute, Cree Lake scored a goal, but then, Prince Albert put up a stellar defence that appeared to stymie Cree Lake. Leading 5-1 with 2:05 left to play, again fans started to file out. Then a fight nearly broke out between Nancy and a Prince Albert player, after Nancy apparently said something to him while they were in a scrum. She refused to raise a hand as he pummelled her mercilessly.

Monte, aware that Cree Lake might come out of this situation with an advantage, frantically restrained his fellow players, as he whispered something to them. He looked over at the coach and smiled. The linesmen pulled the Prince Albert player off Nancy. She got up and skated away, receiving no penalty while the other player got a 5 minute penalty for fighting and a game misconduct. Nancy skated over to the coach and said, "like the way I controlled my temper coach? Pretty cool, don't you think?"

Coach Wellman, curious as to what happened asked very pointedly, "what did you say to him, Nancy?

Nancy, nonchalantly, with a smile creasing her lips, replied, "believe me coach, I am too much of a lady to ever tell you what I said to him. Ask Monte sometime. He is the one who told me what to say."

As the penalty was being assessed, Coach Wellman called his team over to the bench. It was then that another Prince Albert player skated over and challenged a player on the Cree Lake bench to a fight. Wellman held his player back. The referee assessed another double minor penalty to Prince Albert for unsportsmanlike conduct. Prince Albert, down two players was still confident that they could hold on for the victory.

The dark clouds that had obscured the northern lights dissipated, and the rink was bathed in a soft green light that twinkled and shimmered brilliantly on the ice, as the sky seemed to light up with a translucent glow. Penetrating the eerie quiet that had descended all about the rink, the lonely sound of a howling coyote could be heard in the distance.

Coach Wellman pulled the goalie with 2:05 remaining, so in effect, Cree Lake had a three man advantage. Nancy, winning the face-off to the right of the Prince Albert goalie got the puck over to Myrna, who promptly flipped it back to her. The goalie was caught flat-footed, 5-2.

The ensuing face-off at centre ice was won easily by Cree Lake. Again, Myrna was open on the left wing. She took a pin-point pass from Nancy and skated in all alone. 5-3 with 1:47 left to play.

The roar of the crowd was thunderous. The player with the double minor came back on the ice as Ted's line skated out, won the face-off and blasted across the blue line like Patton invading Germany. Ted circled behind the net and found Larry Thundercloud open on the point. He one-timed it into the net, 5-4 with 1:08 left to play.

The methodical, calm demeanour of the Cree Lake team was, no doubt, disconcerting to what was now a confused and bewildered Price Albert team. Again, Cree Lake won the face-off and Myrna streaked behind the Prince Albert net, finding Nancy open on the right side of the goal. She scored uncontested, 5-5 with 41 seconds to play.

The ensuing face-off was sent behind the Badgers net, where Benson Frank, never really a great skater, picked it up and made a weaving and bobbing dash up the ice to the amazement of all. At the Prince Albert blue line, he passed to Nancy, who barely touched the puck as she scooted it over to Myrna who skated behind the net, waiting patiently for her team-mates to crowd the front of the goal. With only seven seconds left she passed to Frank on the point, who saw Nancy wide open to the right of the net. He passed to her and she one timed the puck behind the sprawling goalie. The improbable had occurred. The 6-5 win made the team 35-0 with only one game left.

It is no stretch to say that hockey mania broke out in Cree Lake that evening. Long after the game was over, the players and fans continued to linger at the rink. It was as if everyone involved, but for the Prince Albert team, did not want the euphoria to end. If you go deep into the heart, you will find something missing in all humanity, something not seen, something for which all humans long but cannot define. On that night that emptiness within subsided, as all who witnessed the impossible genuinely felt that their hearts were filled with that indiscernible thing that all of humanity seeks. They could not describe what it was, but the fullness within felt by all who were there swelled up into a deep and abiding pride in the possibilities of life.

On that night, Coach Wellman's wife greeted him after the game with a warm embrace, knowing that for one fleeting moment in the existence of the small corner of the earth known as Cree Lake, the unjust realities of life had been crushed by the possibilities and wonders offered through a group of young Aboriginals triumphantly led by the man she loved. The devoted band of players had found their champion in the coach, and the coach had found his reason for living in them. They believed in him, and he in them.

As the elation continued unabated by so many who lived lives of quiet desperation, it was as if a glittering image of joy had been carved out of shiny marble. The little town was bathed in glorious recognition that sometimes the most improbable of things can occur. The hockey team proved that no matter how impossible or how incredible the odds against success are, there can be a light at the end of a dark tunnel of despair.

Cree Lake had suffered though years of neglect after an oil company tore treasure from the bowels of the land that these most noble of human beings called home. When their desire for profit was satiated and the treasure exhausted, they proved that they had no more morals than a thief in the night. Packing up and leaving a wasteland, where once there was a paradise, these modern day corporate conquerors left the people with lives of depravation and despair. Now, hope was back, hockey mania flowed through the people like a raging river through a gorge.

Saturday afternoon, Cree Lake did not need a dramatic comeback. A thoroughly demoralized Prince Albert team meekly succumbed by a score of 5-0.

Ironically, the star of the game was the towering Grif "Bad Boy" Joe, whom the coach skated out to defend against attacks on Nancy and Myrna by a Prince Albert team that was so despondent over the previous night's loss they decided to lay waste to the Cree Lake team's stars, rather than try and win the game. When it was all over, it was the Prince Albert team that lay wasted and exhausted on the field of battle, courtesy of Grif, who never saw an opposing player he did not want to check with fury. Heads bowed, the Prince Albert team lined up to shake hands, and their captain said, as he shook Nancy Running Elk's hand, "I compliment you on your play, and I have never seen a better example of team effort than you guys exhibited this weekend."

The celebratory mood continued unabated throughout Cree Lake that night and Sunday, but the trial of Tipper Running Bear and Lenny Dan was scheduled to begin on Monday. When that happened, something even more explosive would occur.

CHAPTER 12
ALMOST AS EXCITING AS A HOCKEY GAME, EH

I do not wonder at the evil men do, but I do wonder at their lack of shame for it. (Coach Wellman to his wife, Janice, when discussing the way Aboriginals were treated in North America. Little did they know how apropos it would be to the case of Lenny Dan and Tipper Running Bear.)

For some time, talk in Cree Lake had centred on two things: the hockey team and the general store robbery. Judge Adam Beadlemann came to town once a month to hear cases. This case had been put off so often he was surprised that it was now on the docket. No doubt, there would be a great deal of interest in the trial, so in order to accommodate the crowd, the judge moved it from the police station conference room to the vacant bingo hall on Main Street.

Janice and Wayne Wellman had become convinced of Lenny Dan's innocence; although, they were less sure of Tipper Running Bear's lack of guilt. Consequently, they were in the gallery when the judged slammed down his gavel and announced that court was in session.

The prosecuting attorney had come up from Meadow Lake, and his reputation was that of a no-nonsense legal eagle with a penchant for prosecuting Aboriginals and demanding the maximum penalty in each case. From his stern demeanour, one sensed that he saw everything in a vacuum and there was not any speck of moral ambiguity in the administration of justice. There was no room for sentiment in anything this man did. Everything was either black or white, with no shades of grey.

On the other hand, Dylan Remington, the attorney for Tipper and Lenny, was a tall, craggy, thin man of about 45 who wore old fashioned horned-rimmed glasses that gave him a studious look. His demeanour was more like that of a kindly old minister than that of an attorney. His suit, unlike the high-dollar, immaculately tailored suit worn by the prosecutor, was dishevelled and wrinkled. Still, there was a quiet authority about this man. He exuded, with quiet confidence, the impression that he would stand against any and all inequalities perpetrated upon the disadvantaged in a world where the few ruled with the iron hand of oppression over those living on the margins of society. This was a man who could have practiced his trade on Bay Street in Toronto, representing the moneyed classes and the corporate barons of greed for high dollars. Yet, he plied his trade in the backwater towns and hamlets of Saskatchewan as well as the cities of despair, representing the rogues and marginalized of society who refused to submit to the authoritarian manifestations of those who demanded uniformity and adherence to a set of rules that too often made slaves out of human beings. This was more than a man with a cause. He was a man standing against the tide of uniformity imposed by the wealthy and powerful.

Coach Wellman felt that Remington was like the hockey player who skated onto the ice when all seemed lost. He might lose the battle, but his adversaries would know that he did not go meekly into the night. He would go down fighting.

Remington greeted his two clients with a confident handshake, turned and smiled at Coach Wellman and his wife, acknowledging them for their commitment to justice by arranging through the legal aid society the representation that all accused people justly deserved, but were too often denied. Like many of his cases, this might be a losing cause, but the cause of social and economic justice was worth fighting for in a world where too few people every received any justice at all.

While pretty much everyone in town assumed the two boys guilty of the crime, Coach Wellman and Janice were not sure about it. Besides, even if they were guilty, they were entitled to a fair hearing. Their crime was more overt, but what about the clandestine crimes committed daily by the corporate thieves who continued with impunity to rob and plunder under a system of economic servitude inflicted on all humanity? So-called justice was meted out to the weak and poor, while the rich and powerful were rarely, if ever, held to account.

The opening argument by the prosecutor was direct and to the point. The culprits of a crime netting them nearly $80,000 in loot were the two native men sitting in the court room before a jury that would be duty bound to find them guilty once the irrefutable evidence was presented. One of them had even hidden some of the merchandise stolen in his family's barn, and the other was caught with a cigarette of the brand stolen before there had been any of that brand even distributed in the entire province of Saskatchewan. Case closed – open and shut.

Mr. Remington got up slowly, looked at the judge in a respectful and meek way and launched into a soliloquy that was more than a refutation of the charges. It was an indictment of a justice system that seemed to prey on the weak and vulnerable. This was more than a case of robbery, it was an example of law enforcement directing the investigation toward an outcome they wanted.

In the case of Constable McMillan, he was a man who had for years been harassing both of the accused. This was merely a rush to judgement in order to finally lock-up two young men who had been in his sights for years. There were nefarious and sinister forces at work to railroad these young men into jail for a crime they did not commit, simply because they had committed crimes in the past. A truly fair justice system does not use past transgressions as an excuse to lock-up individuals for a crime they did not commit. In addition, it was well-known that Constable McMillan was intent on arresting a third party, who was a minor, for compliancy in the crime when she had an iron-glad alibi. Pure and simple, these two young men were victims of an over-zealous policeman who was willing to go to any lengths to incarcerate those whom he considered a menace to society.

Although Remington was eloquent beyond measure, it must be said that there were few in the courtroom who genuinely believed the boys innocent. After all, they had been guilty of many misdeeds in the past. Even the coach and his wife, who believed wholeheartedly in Lenny Dan's innocence, still had their doubts about Tipper.

The first witness was store owner, Harold Lasky, who laid out clearly that he had ordered the merchandise to distribute in the spring to his other stores in Northern Saskatchewan, with the intention of keeping only a few items for local sale in Cree Lake. His business was rapidly expanding and he needed a storage facility. He further stated that he had seen Tipper and Lenny in the store when he was discussing the arrival of the merchandise with Constable McMillan. It was obvious that they had overheard the conversation.

In spite of Remington's strenuous objections to the fact that there was no way that Lasky could be sure that the two overheard him and McMillan, the judge ruled the statement admissible.

Then, cross examination began from Remington, and Lasky, who had seemed self-assured when being examined by the prosecutor, appeared a bit nervous.

"So, Mr. Lasky, you are one hundred percent sure that the two defendants overheard you and McMillan talking about the arrival of all that merchandise?"

Lasky, assuredly replied, "you bet they overheard. They were only a few feet from us."

In a cynical tone, Remington said, "are you in the habit of discussing the arrival of large quantities of merchandise in public, so anyone can clearly hear that it is in your store?"

"No, McMillan and I are friends. I was just letting him know, so he would be aware that it would be there for a couple of days. I did not suggest it to him, but I assumed he might keep a more watchful eye on the store."

"Were you aware that McMillan had often accused these boys of nefarious deeds?"

"I suppose so."

"Well, Mr. Lasky, did you think it wise to discuss the arrival of all this merchandise in front of two young men whom Constable McMillan had often accused of being involved in criminal activity?"

"I never really thought about it?"

"I see. You never thought about it. Two people whom you knew had been in occasional trouble with the law and you never thought about it. Of course, you were well insured, were you not?"

Before Lasky could answer, the prosecutor vehemently shouted, "objection your honour! Whether the witness was insured or not has no relevance to the crime that was committed."

Remington calmly looked at the judge and said, "but your honour, it does have relevance, but I cannot connect the relevance until there is another witness on the stand. At that time, the court will see the relevance of the question as it goes directly to motive."

Again, the prosecutor interjected, "what motive your honour? This whole line of questioning is irrelevant and immaterial!"

The judge seemed to contemplate for a second and said, "I am inclined to allow the question. However, Mr. Remington, be assured that I will not allow an unfettered fishing expedition. Objection overruled. Mr. Lasky, you will answer the question."

Lasky, with a note of hesitation in his voice, replied in a voice so low, it was almost a whisper. "Yeah."

Remington leaned in close to the witness. "A little louder so we can all hear Mr. Lasky."

"Yes, yes. I am insured."

"And how much were you insured for Mr. Lasky."

Again, the prosecutor, now seemingly indignant over the direction of the questioning shouted, "objection, your honour. Again, you have allowed the question about whether he was insured or not. The defence counsel is toying with the court's indulgent nature. What difference could it possibly make how much he was insured for? The witness has said he was insured. He has answered the question."

The judge, contemplatively replied, "I have allowed the original question about having insurance, Mr. Remington. I do not see how the amount is relevant. Objection is sustained."

"Very well your honour, but you must understand that my line of questioning is moving toward the real reason a robbery was committed. There are underlying forces in play here that will become abundantly clear as the case progresses, so I ask that the court keep in mind at a later date that the amount of insurance will become relevant when asked of another witness. I would hope for an affirmative ruling at that time."

"So noted Mr. Remington, please continue with your questioning."

Turning toward the two defendants, Mr. Remington pointed directly at them. "These two men have been in your store often have they not, Mr. Lasky?"

"They have. Everyone in town comes into my store. It is the only place they can buy groceries and supplies locally."

With a quizzical look, Mr. Remington asked his next question. "And Mr. Lasky, since you are the only grocery in town, I suppose business is very good."

A now thoroughly frustrated prosecutor yelled, "please, your honour. How long must this go on. Mr. Lasky's business is not on trial here. The state of his business has no bearing whatsoever on this case."

A slight smile creeping across his lips, Mr. Remington interjected a terse comment. "Your honour, it does have relevance, and if I will be allowed some leeway, this line of questioning will become extremely relevant as we get beneath the surface and find out the real reasons this crime was committed. In fact, Mr. Lasky is being a bit disingenuous, as there is, in a manner of speaking, another store in town."

The judge, somewhat perplexed, asked of Mr. Remington, "are you accusing this witness of perjury?"

"Not necessarily your honour, but the truth is that Mr. Lasky does not have the only store in town. If I can be allowed to continue with my line of questioning, I think it will be evident that Mr. Lasky is perhaps not overtly lying about this, but may indeed be guilty of stretching the truth."

Again, the prosecutor strenuously objected. "Your honour, regardless of the answer to the question. It is irrelevant and immaterial. It has nothing to do with the case at hand."

"I am inclined to give Mr. Remington some leeway in light of the fact he thinks he can prove disingenuousness in regards to Mr. Lasky's answer. However, be aware Mr. Remington that you had better be able to substantiate your contentions. The objection is overruled. Continue your questioning Mr. Remington."

At that point, Coach Wellman noticed Lasky, with a concerned look, glance directly at McMillan, who was sitting among the witnesses in the front row behind the prosecutor. There seemed to be a look of desperation on Mr. Lasky's part.

"So, Mr. Lasky – you have the only store in town? Is that completely accurate?"

"I think so. I am aware of no other grocery stores."

"Mr. Lasky, have you had complaints about the high prices you charge?"

Rising quickly, the prosecutor frustratingly cried, "your honour, please. How much longer must we endure this absurd fishing expedition which has no relevance to the matter before the court? I strenuously object."

The judge, now showing some frustration with the line of questioning, was very terse with Remington. "Mr. Remington, I have given you great latitude here, but I am about at the end of my rope. The prices Mr. Lasky charges are irrelevant. Either continue with the line of questioning relating to his veracity in regards to being the only store in town or move on. Objection sustained."

"I apologize to the court your honour, but I am actually trying to save the court some time by having this witness provide information that can be provided by other witnesses, if this individual continues to evade my question. I put it to you again Mr. Lasky, in perhaps a way that will get a more positive response. Are there any others in town who dispense groceries and household supplies other than you?"

Lasky, crossing his legs, seemed a bit nervous now. He even started fidgeting with his watch. "Well, well, I, I, suppose you might consider Louella Running Bear and Francis Dan to be operating somewhat of a store. They go to Wal-Mart in Prince Albert once a month, stock-up on a variety of items ordered by people, and they hire a man to drive a rented van from Prince Albert to Missinipe, where the stuff is loaded on a snow-cat with a sled behind it. When the cat arrives at the Dan farm, the people show up to pick up their items, and they all pay a portion of the transportation costs. Seems like a lot of trouble to me just to save a few dollars."

"I see. So, you are the only genuine store, but you do have competition?"

"If you want to call it that."

"Is it not true that your business has dropped considerably the last year since the Dan's and the Running Bear's have been doing this?"

"Some, I suppose."

"Mr. Lasky. The truth is that my two clients, at the behest of their mothers, are actually driving the truck and the snow-cat, correct?"

"Yeah, I suppose."

"Mr. Lasky, if these two people were in jail, the monthly trips to the Wal Mart in Prince Albert might be curtailed. Would you say that is a fair assumption?"

"Well, I am sure they could find someone else to drive the truck and snow-cat."

"Actually Mr. Lasky, that would be highly unlikely wouldn't it, as you must have a special driving permit to operate a snow-cat. According to the records in the transportation department in Regina, Lenny Dan is the only person in Cree Lake who has a snow-cat approved licence. Sure, someone else could take the course and get one, but it would take awhile, meanwhile, you would be devoid of competition for a good long while wouldn't you?"

Lasky sat silently, aghast at the information Mr. Remington had accumulated. Looking at the judge, Remington said, "obviously, Mr. Lasky does not want to answer the last question. No matter your honour, I think his silence is answer enough. No more questions of this witness."

Those in the courtroom sat in stunned silence. Where was this going? Wayne and Janice Wellman looked at one another quizzically. Were they wrong about Tipper Running Bear? Could he be just as innocent as they assumed Lenny was?

The next witness called by the prosecution was Constable McMillan. He simply laid out the facts of the case against the two men, and then was turned over to Dylan Remington for cross-examination, but it was nearly noon, so the judge adjourned court until 2:00 PM.

During the lunch break, Janice Wellman invited Mr. Remington to her house for lunch. It was during lunch that they were told by Remington that he was about to expose a much more nefarious crime than a mere store robbery. Through the efforts of a private detective named Aaron Adams, who was visiting Remington from New York City, an incredible plot had been uncovered.

Shocked at this revelation, Wayne and Janice eagerly asked about it, but were simply told the truth would come out, and that the key would be something that was unwittingly done by Grif Joe, who would, if needed, be called as a witness to prove that a tangled web of deceit had been woven to convict two innocent young men of a crime that they had planned but never carried out. Remington said, "many times, the answer to a mystery is in plain sight. The answer is so apparent that it just isn't seen. Thanks to the efforts of my friend from New York City, whose propitious visit coincided with my taking this case, the truth was discovered."

That afternoon at 2:00 o'clock a stern-looking, arrogantly confident acting Constable McMillan took the stand for cross-examination.

Just as Remington started his cross-examination with the phrase, "Mr. McMillan," he was interrupted by McMillan who said, "I am generally referred to as Constable McMillan out of respect for my position."

"Oh, forgive me Constable McMillan, I am a product of a family that taught me we are all equal and no one should be exalted over another; therefore, I have always figured the term Mr., Miss. Mrs. or Ms. was adequate respect, rather than using titles to put some people on a higher

126

plane than others. If I met the Prime Minister, I would refer to him as Mr. Harper, not as Mr. Prime Minister, because I figure I and every other Canadian is his equal. However, in your case, your authority and your gun might make me think twice,"

Irate with indignation and anger for what he perceived as utter disrespect, the prosecutor furiously and strenuously objected, "Your honour, please, how much longer will this go on? Does the court have to listen to Mr. Remington debase the sanctity of these proceedings to make social commentary and attack a loyal, dedicated, competent public servant?"

The judge immediately admonished Mr. Remington and told him the court would tolerate no disrespect for a witness, to which Mr. Remington had a tart reply. "Your honour, I think it inappropriate for the prosecutor to state that Mr. McMillan is a loyal, dedicated, competent public servant. That unduly influences the jury. I intend to prove that he is neither dedicated or loyal, and certainly not competent."

Suddenly McMillan stood up in the witness box and shouted directly at Remington. "You mess with me fellow and you are going to be in more trouble than you can handle."

Remington, laughed, looked up to the judge and countered the tirade with a statement that brought a giggle to many in the crowd. "Your honour, I think the court should admonish the witness for threatening the defence attorney. As for his threat. I say, bring it on. I am not a physically imposing man, but I have never backed down from a fight in my life. The rule of law is bigger than the threats of a disgraceful excuse of a police officer who has railroaded two innocent young men."

Suddenly, the prosecutor was again on his feet, frantically shouting his objections to the comments by Remington. Judge Beadleman, outraged at the conduct by the defence attorney and the witness, was pounding furiously with his gavel, demanding order in the court. "Gentleman, I will have none of this. Mr. Remington, any more snide innuendos about the witness from you, and I shall hold you in contempt. Likewise, Constable McMillan, you are hereby warned the same as Mr. Remington, you are boarding on contempt with your threats. I will not tolerate any disrespect for the dignity of this court."

A quiet, uneasy hush fell over the court, as Remington, in a contrite, civil but somewhat snide manner, said "I humbly and contritely apologize to the court, your honour. The rabid defence against injustice sometimes broils up in me so much that I go to the extreme. It will not happen again."

"The court accepts your apology Mr. Remington, but it appears there is a tone of disrespect to it. I, again, admonish you to watch your step. You do not want to trifle with me. I hope that you implicitly understand that you are on a precipice, ready to fall where you don't want to go. Continue with your examination of the witness, please."

With great skill and purpose, Mr. Remington was careful to avoid using the term constable. When he started out with "Mr. McMillan," the witness sit up defiantly in his chair and glared at Remington. Remington continued, "so, you have been a policeman here in Cree Lake for how long?"

"Three years."

Again, with great skill, Mr. Remington was careful to avoid the use of the term constable. "Mr. McMillan, how many arrests have you made in that time?"

"Hundreds. Who knows."

"Well, actually, Mr. McMillan, I know." He held up a paper and continued. "According to this document from the Criminal Statistics Division in Regina, you have made 683 arrests in the 34 months you have been here. And I stress that is the arrests in which it was recorded that you were the arresting officer. There are three men on the force here, and the other two men combined, have only made 82 arrests during those 34 months. In fact, Mr. McMillan, you have arrested my client, Lenny Dan, 7 times during that period, and you have arrested Tipper Running Bear 6 times. You genuinely like arresting people don't you?"

"I arrest people when they break the law. That is what I am hired to do."

"Well, Mr. McMillan, you certainly are zealous about your job. In fact, it appears you are so incredibly zealous that you have accumulated over seven times the number of arrests when compared to the other two officers in Cree Lake combined.

The prosecutor interrupted, "your honour, I object to this line of questioning. Where is this going?"

The judge, becoming somewhat concerned that he was losing control of the trial, said, "Mr. Remington, get on with it. If you have a point to make with this witness, make it and make it quick."

"Yes, your honour, I shall do just that. Mr. McMillan, do you have a particular grudge against Aboriginals?"

The now extremely frustrated prosecutor rose, shaking his head in disgust. "Objection your honour. This line of examination is completely beyond the pale."

Mr. Remington directed his remarks at the judge. "Your honour, the question goes to motive for the arrest of my clients. I am connecting the arrests to extreme prejudice on the part of the witness, who had a preconceived notion of their guilt and never really considered that anyone else might have committed the crime, in spite of the fact that I will present evidence that he knew someone else committed it. My clients are entitled to a vigorous defence based upon all available facts in relation to their arrests. The prosecutor is more concerned with protecting the integrity of the witness than getting at the truth."

"Point well taken, Mr. Remington. Objection overruled. Continue with your questioning."

"You have any idea what the population of Cree Lake is, Mr. McMillan?"

"About 1200."

"1205 to be exact, Mr. McMillan, of which, according to the Bureau of Statistics at the capitol, 80% are Aboriginal. Consequently, it might make sense that at least 80% of the arrests made by the police would likely be Aboriginal. Ironically, about 80% of the arrests made by your fellow officers have been Aboriginal. However, what is your Aboriginal arrest percentage, Mr. McMillan?"

"I have no idea, I don't look at the colour of the skin when I arrest someone. You break the law, you get arrested."

"Well, Mr. McMillan, what if I told you that in your arrest records, which are a matter of public record, 100% of them were Aboriginals?"

McMillan simply sat and stared at Remington.

"Mr. McMillan, again I ask you, would you be surprised that 100% of your arrests were Aboriginals?"

McMillan's disgust and contempt for Remington was obvious as his face turned beet red and he shouted, "so what? They break the law more. They get arrested more."

"I see. So Aboriginals, according to you, have a greater propensity to break the law?"

"Look's that way doesn't it?"

"Well, I won't answer that Mr. McMillan. I would like to, but I am sure that the prosecutor would object, because my answer would involve a litany of things that are wrong with the economic and social justice systems in this country and others throughout the imperfect world in which we live. Nonetheless, let's move on to the discussion you had with Mr. Lasky about the impending arrival of $80,000 worth of merchandise to his store for storage until it could be distributed throughout Northern Saskatchewan. Were you aware that Lenny Dan and Tipper Running Bear were in the store at the time of the discussion?"

"Well, I know there were a lot of people in the store. I may remember them being there, I can't say with a high degree of certainty that they were there."

"Mr. McMillan, you are a highly trained police officer. I would think you are always highly cognizant of who and what is around at any given time. Suppose I tell you that I can produce three witnesses who say they saw you follow the defendants into the store? Would that perhaps jog your memory a bit?

"O.K., O.K. I guess I remember them. So what?"

"So what? Well, isn't it strange that you would follow the defendants into the store, go over to Mr. Lasky in front of them and discuss the arrival of all that merchandise while in ear-shot of the defendants when you considered them nefarious individuals?"

"Hey, Mr. Lasky brought it up."

"True, but you could have moved away to a more private place, or at lest lowered your voices. According to the people I have talked with, you and Mr. Lasky were quiet loud, making it possible for everyone in the store to hear about it. Was that just a lapse of probity, or did you want everyone to hear about it?"

"What are you getting at?"

"Mr. McMillan, I am just stating a fact that will be corroborated by at least three witnesses to whom my investigator talked. You and Mr. Lasky were less than discrete about the arrival of the merchandise. It was almost as if you wanted the two defendants to hear you, and at the same time, make sure that the others in the store also heard you speak loud enough for the defendants to hear about the merchandise."

"Preposterous. I am an officer of the law. I do not expect to have my integrity questioned."

"Actually Mr. McMillan, you do have to have your integrity questioned. That is my duty as an attorney – to question the motives of those who are trying to railroad my clients into jail."

The prosecutor had sat silently for as long as he could. "Your honour, I object to this line of questioning – to this line of attack. This is nothing more than a public castigation of law enforcement. Mr. Remington has no shame, and he will go to any lengths to impugn the reputation of this dedicated public official."

"Mr. Remington, I am inclined to agree with the prosecutor. Unless you can convince me that this line of questioning is leading somewhere, I will have to sustain the objection."

It was subtlety obvious that Mr. Remington was thoroughly enjoying the sparring with the prosecutor and the judge. Coach Wellman could not help but smile, as he sensed that Mr. Remington was like a hockey player who kept needling an opponent just to get that extra edge on the ice. Remington was a master craftsman in the courtroom, and watching him was a pleasurable experience.

Remington looked pensively at the judge and said, "your honour, this witness is obviously hostile toward the defendants. I think it is also obvious that he is hostile toward me, and if given some leeway by the court, I am about to prove that this entire episode leading to the arrest of the defendants is nothing more than a well-orchestrated, nefarious exercise to railroad these young men to rid the community of what Mr. McMillan sees as a menace, while allowing the real culprits to escape justice. I am not questioning the integrity of law enforcement in general, but I am questioning the integrity of one law enforcement officer in particular. Justice is never served by allowing those in authority to administer justice when, where, how and in any way they see fit. Justice is served by making sure that those who enforce the law, also follow the law."

"Very eloquent Mr. Remington, I am inclined to agree with you. Consequently, I shall overrule the objection. Continue with your questioning, and Mr. McMillan, I also admonish you to avoid being overtly hostile. This court expects all witnesses to conduct themselves with the proper decorum, and that particularly applies to witnesses who should know better by virtue of their positions."

"Thank you, your honour. Now, Mr. McMillan, we know that for some time these two men have been under constant scrutiny by law enforcement here in Cree Lake. Yet, your fellow officers have never had occasion to arrest them. Yet, for some reason you have arrested them a total of 13 times combined. Would you say that is a bit unusual?"

"No, it is just the way it is."

"So, it just appears that when these boys do something deemed illegal, you are always the one on duty or present to observe the illegal activity?"

"It happens that way sometimes."

"I see. Well, could you tell me about finding some of the merchandise that was stolen in Lenny Dan's barn. You got a warrant to search his place right away. Why would you immediately suspect him?"

"He is always at the top of the suspect list. He is constantly in trouble, so it should be obvious that he would be considered a suspect."

"In other words, if there is a crime committed, Lenny Dan is always on the suspect list."

"That isn't unusual in law enforcement. We learn early on that most crimes are committed by what would be termed repeat offenders. Lenny Dan and Tipper Running Bear fit that profile."

"Well, Mr. McMillan, I would actually agree with you there. I think statistics would probably support that contention. It appears we finally agree on something. However, statistics do not take into account the factors that sometimes drive people to crime like poverty, lack-of-opportunity and harassment from those in authority. Putting that aside, could you tell the court why you went out to Lenny Dan's place with a search warrant. Isn't it usual procedure to question someone first to explore probable cause, before getting a search warrant?"

Just as McMillan was about to answer, Grif, Ted, Monte and Nancy walked into the courtroom. Obviously, school had let out, and they were interested in seeing how Lenny and Tipper were faring. Anyway, there was a rumour that Grif was going to be called to the stand.

Temporarily distracted by the opening and closing door, McMillan was now ready to render an answer to the question. "Well, I have been known to get a search warrant before pre-interviewing the suspect. This was just one of those times I decided to do it first."

"Could you tell the court why you immediately searched the barn first, rather than the house? Isn't it normal procedure to search the house first?"

"Sometimes you search one place. Sometimes you search another. It all depends."

"I see, it all depends on whether or not you actually know where the stolen goods are?"

It was obvious that McMillan was getting nervous. Yet, he managed to maintain his arrogant demeanour. "I don't know what you mean by that. I am not some kind of psychic. How would I have known where the stolen goods were unless I looked?"

"Well, Mr. McMillan, that will be evident in due time. Let us move to another detail. We know you searched Lenny Dan's place almost immediately and came upon some of the merchandise with relative ease. I noticed that you were rather observant of the arrival a few minutes ago of Grif Joe. He was actually critical to your apprehension of Tipper Running Bear was he not?"

"He provided a valuable clue for us, yes."

"And what was that clue?"

"It was a cigarette butt picked up by him at the Upton place, where Tipper was doing some work. He threw the cigarette down in the snow. Grif Joe found it, brought it to me, and since it was a Chesterfield cigarette, which had never been distributed here in town, it connected Tipper to the robbery. Pretty simple deduction. Furthermore, when we arrested Tipper Running Bear, he had about a half smoked pack of Chesterfield's in his pocket. Pretty cut and dried."

Remington scratched his head with his right hand, paced over to where Lenny and Tipper were sitting, turned back toward McMillan and said, "well, that is true except for one thing Mr. McMillan. Tipper smoked the cigarette. He threw it into the snow. He even put the half-empty pack in his pocket. However, that does not prove that they were his cigarettes. Is it possible that he could have found the pack of cigarettes on the lip of the white fence that enclosed the Upton's front yard?"

A thoroughly disgusted McMillan stared daggers at Remington. "Well, almost anything is possible, but I doubt it in this case."

Again scratching his head and tussling his already unruly hair, Remington leaned in close to McMillan. "Did you go out to the Upton farm the day Grif Joe found that cigarette?"

"I go a lot of places in the course of the day. How could I remember whether I went there or not?"

"Well, my client will attest that he saw you there. Of course, we know that you do not put much credence in what my client says, so if you can't remember, when I start calling my witnesses, I am sure Grif Joe will testify that, as he was walking to the Upton home, he saw you drive past him on the road. Now you may not have been going to the Upton home, as there are many other places you could have gone on that road. However, there is Mrs. Upton who happened to look out he window when you stopped to talk with the defendant, Tipper Running Bear. I can also call her to testify. Of course, given these details, perhaps now you can recall visiting my client that day at the Upton home."

"Yeah, yeah, I recall that I did drop by to see him."

Grinning slightly, you could tell that Dylan Remington felt he was on a roll. "Kind of funny isn't it Mr. McMillan that you would send Grif Joe to deliver a package to the Uptons, when you were going out there anyway?"

Somewhat hesitant, McMillan stuttered as he said, "I, I forgot that I needed to see Tipper about the robbery."

"Oh really. So, why didn't you stop and pick-up Grif when you passed him? After all, you knew he was going right where you were going, and you knew he had the package. Hey, you could have just picked up the package and sent him back. That way he could have made it to hockey practice on time. I know Coach Wellman would have appreciated that."

Now, obviously getting terribly concerned about the direction the questioning was going, McMillan looked at Lasky, who was sitting in the front row of the courtroom, almost as to plead for some help. "I, I, well, I guess I just wasn't thinking straight at the time. I had my mind on solving the robbery."

"How commendable of you Mr. McMillan. I can certainly understand your devotion to duty. I feel the same way when I am convinced my clients are being railroaded."

Having sat quietly, the prosecutor could not let that statement about railroading go by without an objection. "Your honour, here we go. He isn't asking questions, he is editorializing for his clients. That statement is entirely inappropriate, immaterial and irrelevant."

The judge, who had been giving Remington a great deal of leeway, was beginning to see the holes in the case, but he felt that the objection was well-founded. "Mr. Remington, you will refrain from your scathing comments that are not based on fact."

"Sorry, your honour. Sometimes I do get a little over zealous in defence of my clients."

"Fine, please continue your cross-examination."

"How long did you talk to Mr. Running Bear?"

"A few minutes, I just warned him that it would be better if he came clean about the robbery, as the sentence would be lighter if he admitted to it."

"So, you drove all the way out there just for that?'

"Yes."

"Did you get out of your car?"

"Yes, Tipper was standing by the gate, shovelling snow, so I got out, walked over to where he was working and spoke to him."

"So, you stood by the fence?"

"Yes."

"And there was a 2X5 lip on the inside of the fence was there not?"

"I don't recall."

"I see. Well, there is a 2x4 lip on the top of the fence. Strange you don't recall that, because when my client put down his shovel and walked over to you, he noticed your hand on the lip. Then after you left, there was a half empty pack of Chesterfield cigarettes on the lip of the fence."

"That's his story. I already have heard from him during interrogation that he found the cigarettes at the Upton's house. Grif brought in the smoked cigarette butt, and Tipper knew we had him, so he just made up the story about finding the pack of smokes."

"I see, just another lie from a lad whom you had many run-ins with over the years you have been here in Cree Lake. Mr. McMillan, you were extremely adamant in your belief that these two young men committed the robbery, and that they were aided and abated by a young lady named Nancy Running Elk. Is that a fair assumption?"

"Yes, but I could never get any concrete evidence on Nancy Running Elk. Besides, she had someone who gave her an iron-glad alibi."

"That is correct. Her alibi is a Mr. and Mrs. Wilton, I believe. Yet, you still have reason to suspect her?"

"Yes. First Mrs. Wilton is known by everyone in town to be mentally challenged ever since her son up and disappeared three years ago. As for Mr. Wilton, I do not know why he would give her an alibi. I believe he is just mistaken about the time. Those two boys aren't smart enough to pull this off themselves, and she is a known associate of theirs and she is cunningly smart."

"Sheriff, may I ask if you have on your bullet proof vest?"

The prosecutor was livid, as he shouted, "objection, your honour. I simply can no longer sit here as this man makes a mockery of this court. You are allowing him to absolutely impugn the integrity of this witness with no restraint whatsoever. His questions are so wide-ranging that they have no relevance to this case."

"Oh, your honour, they do have great relevance. If I will be allowed to connect the dots, I will blow holes so wide in this case you could sail an aircraft carrier through them."

"Mr. Remington, I am anxious to see if you can do that. Objection overruled."

"Thank you, your honour. Now, Mr. McMillan, do you have your bullet proof vest on?"

141

"Of course, I always wear it."

"Even when out of uniform?"

"Yes, I am a known police officer, and, as such, even when I am off-duty I may have to stop a crime. I only remove my vest when I am at home."

"I see, so even if you were, let's say wearing a white hoodie over your head and a dark jacket, you would have your bullet proof vest on."

Nancy and Monte looked at each other with astonishment, because they knew where Remington was going with this. Nancy even looked down at her hands, realizing why the man who accosted her had such a hard chest. At the same time, Coach Wellman and his wife turned their heads and looked at Monte and Nancy with an intense, all-knowing glare.

"I don't know what that has to do with anything, but, yes, I said I always wear it when I go out."

"I see, and if anyone hits you while you are in it, they would probably hurt their hands, correct?"

You could see the anger well-up in McMillan and in the front row of the courtroom, Lasky looked extremely nervous and agitated.

Nancy could almost feel her hands aching, just as they did the night she pounded on the assailant's chest that seemed to be encased in steel. Her fear, not just for herself, but for a tiny daughter who was frantically screaming in hysteria, had brought horror she had never known but once before in her life. And that previous horror suddenly came cascading back into her memory, as she stood next to Monte in the courtroom – the horror of something even more fearful than being accosted on the road that night. That other unmitigated, horrible night of evil had been locked up in her for years, as she felt unable to share it because of the damage it would do. It was a horror that haunted her and the only two other people who knew about it. When would the three of them ever be free of the secret that bound them together in eternal fear of discovery?

She looked over at Monte, and he gave her a knowing smile of compassion. He reached down and took her hand to silently console her. He thought that it was her realization of who had attacked her that night that made her tremble, but it was not the horror of being accosted on the road that night that was causing the trepidation. It was the recollection of an untold event three years ago that was making her realize that one single occurrence can forever alter one's life.

As Monte sympathetically held her hand, she could feel his warmth and concern emanating from deep within. If only she could tell him the truth. If only she could share with him what she harboured in silent fear, maybe some of the pain would subside. But alas, what would his awareness of what happened do to alter the agonizing reality of three people who suffered in a cold silence of denial and shame for an act of violence?

McMillan, the arrogant, bombastic authoritarian enforcer of the law, sat in fear of each new question that came from the indomitable champion of justice, Dylan Remington. One could sense the deteriorating mental faculties of McMillan, as Remington steadily unravelled a sinister plot to not only plunder for gain, but to lay waste to two young men, simply because they were, as Aboriginals, easy prey and deemed expendable. McMillan and his arrogance were about to be laid bare on the altar of light promulgated by a man who refused to bow before injustice and deceit.

Again, leaning in close to McMillan, as if to say he had no fear of him, Remington continued to dismantle the wall of invincibility that McMillan thought would protect him from retribution. "Can you explain why you and Mr. Lasky followed Coach Wellman the day he left Lenny Dan's place?

"I didn't follow Wellman. I may have been out on the road where he was, but I didn't follow him."

"So, you were not concerned about Wellman getting Lenny Dan out of jail, so he might be free to explore how some of the merchandise from the robbery wound up under the floor of his barn? That he might talk to a local itinerant named Bob George who happened to be walking down the old service road behind the Dan family barn and noticed a police car parked behind the barn just an hour before you showed up with a warrant to search the Dan place?"

McMillan's nervousness became more pronounced, and he struggled to answer the question. "I, I, don't have any idea what you are talking about."

"Of course you don't Mr. McMillan. O.K., let's get back to Nancy Running Elk. You tried to connect her to the robbery didn't you?"

"Of course, I had the evidence on Lenny and Tipper, but she had an alibi. Mr. and Mrs. Wilton said she was at their place, but Mrs. Wilton has been mentally incompetent since her son disappeared three years ago, and Mr. Wilton, well, he is just probably confused about the time. Lenny and Tipper are thieves, no doubt about that, but Nancy is the smart one. She is the one who planned it. I am sure." And then he uttered the phrase that sealed his fate, "and you can take that to the bank."

Suddenly, Lasky leaped to his feet, realizing that the jig was up when McMillan repeated the words that had been overheard by Lenny and Tipper. He struggled to the aisle, and as he started running toward the door, he stumbled and fell. Remington turned to the judge and said, "I suggest you have Mr. Lasky" and then he said McMillan's name with an emphasis on the part McMillan revered so much, "and C-o-n-s-t-a-b-l-e McMillan detained to explain how they stole the $80,000 worth of merchandise, sold it to a third party, planted evidence pointing to my clients and defrauded the insurance company out of $80,000."

The judge said, "bailiff, have Constable McMillan and Mr. Lasky placed in custody. Meanwhile, this court will impose a continuance in the trial of Mr. Dan and Mr. Running Bear until certain matters can be investigated."

Remington confidently walked to his clients, shook their hands, and then he turned to coach Wellman and smiled. "Almost as exciting as a hockey game, eh?"

CHAPTER 13
YES. HE WANTED TO WEEP

The following days were filled with preparations for the Northern Saskatchewan Regional Championship Tournament in Prince Albert that weekend. The team would win all four games without allowing a goal to be scored against them and remain the only undefeated midget team in all of Canada. Qualifying for the Provincial Championship the following weekend in Saskatoon, made the news of the dismissal of charges against Lenny Dan and Tipper Running Bear, and the indictment of McMillan and Lasky seem somewhat unimportant in a village consumed with hockey mania.

Lasky had agreed to plead guilty and testify against McMillan in lieu of a lighter sentence. The Great Northern Grocery chain, agreed to take over Lasky's general store, and Lenny and Tipper had vowed to never get in any trouble again. Most people took their declaration of fidelity to the law with considerable scepticism, but as Coach Wellman said, "I take them at their word, but words are easier than deeds."

Meanwhile, on Monday at school, as they were waiting for the morning bell, Ted and Monte were having a discussion about all the exciting things that had happened in their dull little town the past few months. Ted, who had for sometime been the steady companion of Myrna St. John, asked Monte why he had never asked Nancy for a date?

Surprised at the question, Monte acted perturbed. "Haven't I told you enough. I am not interested in her that way. Nancy is just a friend."

Ted replied, "yeah, sure Monte. That is why every time you are around her I see that little glint in your eye. Anyone can see that your hormones are dancing a jig every time she smiles at you. She really excites you and you know it."

"Get real, Ted. She has a two year old child. Even if I was interested, it is obvious Jasmine comes first with her."

"Yeah, and that is one of the reasons you like her. She has her priorities in order. She is an incredibly responsible mother, and you find that very appealing, because she is more mature than you or me. Heck she is more mature than you and me put together. Not many people 17 years old are as mature and well-grounded as Nancy. I still can't believe how we misjudged her for so long."

Monte with a contemplative look seemed in deep thought. "Yeah, I hope we have learned about judging people. Maybe you and I are maturing a little, too. One thing does still bother me, though."

"What's that?"

"I'd still like to know why she goes out to the Wilton's every Monday evening with Jasmine in tow. Mrs. Wilton is not in her right mind, everyone knows that and ever since her son disappeared, she has gotten worse. And, Mr. Wilton, although nice, is one of the weirdest characters in town. What is her attraction to them?"

Ted, as the bell rang and he turned to head off to class, cavalierly said, "so, why don't you go out there with her and find out what goes on?"

147

Not replying, Monte stood for a second and whispered to himself, "yeah, I might just do that, but not with Nancy."

After hockey practice Monday night, Monte asked Nancy if she was going to the Wilton's. She replied that she and Jasmine always went to the Wilton's on Monday nights between 6:30 until Jasmine's bedtime at 8:30. She seemed curious as to why Monte would ask the obvious, as she had told him many times that Mondays were reserved for visits to the Wilton's. She wondered if he was perhaps wanting to spend some time with her. After all, she knew that Monte was interested in her, but she had long ago vowed that she would never get romantically involved with anyone until Jasmine was much older. Despite the fact that everyone assumed she and Lenny Dan were romantically involved, the truth was that they were nothing more than friends. She knew most people assumed she was a lose woman and gave herself freely to one and all. In fact, Nancy was probably the most chaste girl in town. Yet, she did not care what people thought. Well, most people, she did care what Monte thought.

As they parted company, Monte, who had formulated a plan to find out what was up with the Monday visits to the Wilton's, sequestered himself outside Nancy's home and waited patiently for 6:30 to arrive. He would clandestinely follow her and Jasmine, rather than wait for them to arrive at the Wilton's, because possibly she was stopping off somewhere else first. Did she, maybe, have a boyfriend she was visiting, instead of the Wilton's? The thought made Monte's stomach queasy. No, no, Nancy wouldn't be doing that, would she? Would she? Would she?

The thought of Nancy with someone else nauseated Monte. Yet, he knew she had to have been with someone else. After all, there was Jasmine as living proof of that. He found himself wanting to be her protector, wanting to keep her from pain and harm.

As Nancy and Jasmine walked out of their house, the cold of the winter was gently fading into the spring, but the cold of the north took a long time to morph into warmth. Yet, Monte always felt a warm, intoxicating glow all about, when he was in the presence of Nancy. It was as if he was in a dream, but he recalled once thinking when he was awakening from a dream that perhaps what we termed reality was really a dream and that what we believed to be a dream, was, in fact, reality.

> Take this kiss upon the brow!
> And, in parting from you now,
> Thus much let me avow-
> You are not wrong, who deem
> That my days have been a dream;
> Yet if hope has flown away
> In a night, or in a day,
> In a vision, or in none,
> Is it therefore the less gone?
> All that we see or seem
> Is but a dream within a dream.

> I stand amid the roar
> Of a surf-tormented shore,
> And I hold within my hand
> Grains of the golden sand-
> How few! yet how they creep
> Through my fingers to the deep,
> While I weep- while I weep!

O my! can I not grasp
Them with a tighter clasp?
O my! can I not save
One from the pitiless wave?
Is all that we see or seem
But a dream within a dream?

As Monte followed far back from the two ghost like figures walking down the desolate road, he was absorbed in the moment. Yet, as a slight, gentle breeze began to penetrate the stillness of the bleak, foreboding night, he felt uneasy about what he might find out. Did he really want to solve the dark mystery of Nancy Running Elk? Or, was that part of her mystique that made her seem so alluring?

He wondered at the shallow existence of so many in a world filled with those who, like Constable McMillan, perceived that what was on the surface was simple, permanent, reliable, and of one essence. Monte had come to realize that people led myriad lives and had a variety of sensations, that they were complex creatures that bore within themselves strange legacies, thoughts and passions, and whose very flesh was tainted with the monstrous maladies of experiences that those who were on the outside looking in, simply could not comprehend. He had judged Nancy harshly, because he could not see the real girl who obviously was hiding a dark secret that permeated her very existence. Did he really want to do this? Did he really want to know what the mystery of Nancy Running Elk was all about?

There was an intense fascination with these two lonely, shadowy figures moving majestically and deliberately down the dark road that led to the Wilton's. Monte saw them as shades of mystery in the darkness, and as he watched Nancy gently tugging on the diminutive Jasmine, they both troubled his imagination. Monte had been hypnotically fascinated by a young women who was an enigma. He had begun to look upon Nancy simply as a mode through which he could realize his conception of the truly beautiful, not just in physical form but deep within.

Arriving at the Wilton's, Nancy and Jasmine were greeted at the door by Mr. Wilton, who bent down and swept Jasmine up in his arms. Finding an inconspicuous place behind a dead tree, Monte could see into the brightly lit living room through the curtain-less window. Mr. Wilton took Jasmine over to his wife, and she bent forward, took her into her arms and gently kissed her. Placing her down onto the floor, Jasmine began to play with some toys that were apparently put out for her pleasure. Mrs. Wilton, through her mental aguish, seemed to find a bit of joy in watching the playful little girl, while Nancy disappeared into the kitchen for some time, before returning with what appeared to be hot tea. As they sat and drank the tea, Monte noticed that Mrs. Wilton continued to be her generally stoic self, rarely participating in the conversation, but she did seem more animated and to be showing more of an interest in what was going on around her than usual.

Monte thought to himself that this was just a typical domestic scene, but, still, there was something sinister percolating just beneath the surface. There was a mysterious and dark undercurrent abiding in all those in the little bungalow. They were harbouring a secret, but what was it? Even outside, as Monte hunkered down behind the tree to shield himself from view, he felt an intense uneasiness, almost as if someone or something was watching him, as he gazed inquisitively at those inside.

The gentle wind began to whistle through the trees that were devoid of life in the still lingering winter, and the clouds floating above converged, blurting out the last vestige of pale moonlight that was visible. There was no sound, except the lonely, desperate moaning of the wind.

It felt as if the tongues of terror were about to unleash themselves with a verbal barrage that would shake the very foundations of all those trapped in this dark and lonely place that seemed to harbour some malevolent force that was just waiting to weave itself into the fabric of discontent that abounded. Monte waited, but what was he waiting for in this seemingly disquieted cornucopia of loneliness and despair?

Standing there, now shivering, not from the cold, but from the mounting apprehension that something terrifying was about to happen, Monte asked himself if he was going mad? Under fear of what seemed a coming doom, he resigned himself to doing what he must to once and for all solve the mystery that was Nancy Running Elk.

It was nearly 8:00 o'clock now. Monte had seen nothing that would give any indication of what the dark secret was being hidden beneath the veneer of respectability playing out before him. Why had he followed her? Why did he long to know the truth about Nancy? Then, the curtain was pulled back and the real play began.

Mrs. Wilton got up, was handed a coat by Nancy, who helped her put it on. Nancy put on her own coat, and they waved good-bye to Mr. Wilton and Jasmine. They exited the door and stood on the porch for awhile, as Mrs. Wilton looked stoically and sadly from side-to-side. Nancy, taking Mrs. Wilton's left arm, helped her step into the yard. They turned to the left and started walking down the lane beside the house, toward a grove of honeysuckle trees with barren branches that seemed to be begging for the coming spring that would offer bright red flowering blossoms of beauty in this lonely place that seemed to cry out in pain, anguish and despair.

Clandestinely creeping along behind them, hiding in the darkness of the sullen night behind tree after tree, Monte wondered where they were going. They were not just out for a walk, as there was purpose in their strides. They knew their destination. The darkness seemed to close in around them, and Monte kept looking over his shoulder. Was someone following him? He felt an uneasiness like none he had ever experienced before. He was not afraid to admit it. He was terrified. Was the shadow of death waiting in the darkness that seemed to be calling the two women into its midst?

At the end of the lane was a tall, lifeless tree, a horror of emptiness. The two stopped and just stood there, staring at it. Monte moved a bit to his right, perpendicular to the two women. He was behind a series of leafless shrubs that effectively hid him. The wind began to pick up slightly and the branches of the bushes slapped against his face. He put his cheeks between the braches and gazed in amazement as the two women continued to stand there.

Monte had not looked to the ground in front of the two, but when he finally did, he knew the reason they were there. On the ground was a rectangle the size of a bed, formed by rocks neatly laid out one beside the other. Nancy put her arm around Mrs. Wilton, as she sobbed sorrowfully. She had known where her son was all along. This place was a grave – the grave of James Wilton.

The two women turned to go back home. Mrs. Wilton with her head bowed, the tears still cascading down her cheeks as she woefully sobbed, and Nancy with her right arm consolingly wrapped around the mother of the boy who lay in the cold ground among the grove of trees that seemed like monuments to loneliness and sorrow.

Nancy glanced to her left and saw the shining, penetrating eyes of Monte staring through the leafless bushes. She immediately recognized who it was from the jacket he had on. She said nothing. She raised her left index finger to her lips as if to say "hush," so that Mrs. Wilton would not know he was there.

Monte stood in silence and watched the two of them move slowly up the lane, Mrs. Wilton still sobbing. He stepped from behind the bushes and looked down at the rectangle made by rocks at the base of the tree. There was a sadness to the place, as he stood silent in front of the grave. No name of the deceased carved in stone, it seemed so lonely there at the end of the lane. The now cold, gentle breeze made the leafless branches of the bushes sway to and fro. Obscure clouds overcast the sky, restraining any light on the cold, hard ground that held James Wilton. Mystic, evil-looking shapes seemed to be forming and shimmering in the darkness on the tree, filling Monte with fear and thoughts of how alone James' mother must have felt, knowing her son was gone. Yet, she sat in her home or on her porch, awaiting his return, or was she awaiting a journey, her journey at life's end to join him in his solitary confinement in the shivering horrification of the cold earth that was his home for eternity?

Suddenly, snowflakes began to fall, dancing lightly all about. Monte could not help but wonder why James Wilton was here, rather than in the town cemetery. Had he been buried clandestinely? Ironically, it was not just he who was buried. His mom was living a life of the walking dead, as she pined for a son she loved. She had buried herself in sorrow. Her son may have taken his last breath on this earth, but his last was also hers. She, too, longed for the grave. It was obvious in the way she lived her life.

Monte thought to himself that he would wait for Nancy out on the road. Hopefully, she would share with him the story behind the disappearance of James Wilton and the grave that was at the end of the lane among the grove of honeysuckle trees. Monte turned his back to the grave and left the sad and lonely place, and he, like Mrs. Wilton, wanted to weep. Yes, he wanted to weep.

CHAPTER 14
SOLVING THE MYSTERY

Coming out of the house by herself, Nancy stood on the porch for a second, looking for Monte. Down the road about 100 metres (109 yards), Monte observed her looking for him, so he stepped to the centre of the road and waved. Acknowledging him by raising her hand, Nancy proceeded down the road toward him.

Watching Nancy was an experience of visual delight thought Monte, as she strode toward him down the frozen, hard, tundra-like, empty road. Although short and a bit muscular for a woman, she walked with an incredible air of carefree confidence that made her seem much taller. He could see her dark brown eyes glittering, as the clouds above parted just enough for a ray of light to shine down from the upper crescent of the moon. It almost gave her a halo effect with the light dancing about her head. Could this young lady of whom he had been so disdainful in the past actually be an angel?

As she got closer, Monte gleefully observed her soft face with rounded, high cheek bones, proportionally slim nose, thick dark eyebrows, soft pouted red lips and a rounded chin that complimented that mischievous smile that started in the left corner of her mouth and gradually and charmingly grew wider. Wondrous cascades of love swelled up in Monte.

There was a hint of a wildness lingering behind those softly fluttering eyelids. Nancy's long, silky hair flickered and bounced with each stride, beautifully unkempt and shining brilliantly, framing her soft, gentle face; the mane glimmered down over her shoulders where it rested in regal glory. The uniform hair seemed to beckon for the touch of a loving hand, and Monte found himself longing to rest his head in the softness of her hair and smell its sweetness.

Nancy had a soft neck and narrow but strong shoulders that formed into equally lithe arms and hands, all complimented by a toned, hourglass figure defining her chest and gently swaying hips. As she finally stood there in front of Monte, he wanted to reach out and embrace her. He had embraced many girls in his 17 years, but why could he not bring himself to wrap his arms around Nancy and taste her sweet lips?

Nancy softly said, "come Monte, you can walk me home and I will share something with you that only two other people in the world know. You will be shocked, maybe even think ill of me. I hope not."

"What about Jasmine?"

"She is spending the night with the Wilton's, as she often does. They get great joy out of having her with them, now that their son is gone."

As they walked down the road together, Monte felt a surge of curiosity. He was about to finally get to the bottom of a perplexing mystery.

"First Monte, I must share this with you, not just because you, no doubt, have figured out what lies in the ground out there in the honeysuckle grove, but also, because I have grown to respect you over the past few months, and I am weary of the burden of secrecy. I hope when you hear the story that you will never reveal it to anyone, because if it were known, many people's lives would be adversely affected."

"Nancy, you can rely on my discretion. If you ask my confidentiality, I shall dutifully honour your request."

"Three years ago Monte, I was walking alone on this very road, coming back from Chief Thundercloud Pond, where I had been skating. The darkness crept up on me quickly, and before I knew it, the sun was gone. As I got near the Wilton's house, I sensed that someone was following me, just like I did tonight when Jasmine and I were walking out here."

Monte got a sheepish look on his face as she continued. "Yes, I sensed we were being followed tonight, but I had no idea it was you, but frankly, now I am glad, because I have held this inside for too long, and there is no one I trust more to share it with than you."

She smiled at Monte and went on with her account of what happened to her that night on the road. "I was not really afraid that night, but, for some reason, I felt very uncomfortable. About 100 metres from the Wilton's house, a dark figure came running down the road. Rather than run, I turned to face the figure, and to my surprise it was James Wilton. Well, I knew James, not well, but I knew him, so I was not particularly alarmed. I just figured he was in a hurry to maybe tell me something or to get to his house. You can imagine my surprise when he grabbed me, put his hand over my mouth and started dragging me toward the Wilton's barn."

Monte, now mesmerized by the story Nancy was sharing could only utter, "and?"

"Well Monte, I will not go on with the minute details other than to say that he got me into the barn and warned me that if I screamed he would bash me in the mouth. His hulking size certainly made me realize that I had little chance to overcome him physically, so I decided that I would try and reason with him and reassure him that if he let me go, there would be no repercussions, as I would keep quiet about what had happened. He laughed, threw me on a stack of hay, ripped my clothes off, and I am sure you know what happened after that. Afterward, as I lay on the hay, sobbing uncontrollably, he stood over me, and although I had been frightened before, at that time I sensed that it was all over for me. He reached down in a stall and picked up a bailing hook. I knew that my days were at an end. Surprisingly, I did not cry-out. In fact, I turned on my back and told him to go ahead. I am too much of a lady to tell you the names I called him, but I know it enraged him even more, but, at that point, I figured I was dead anyway."

Monte, his blood boiling with indignation for what Nancy had experienced at the hands of the brutish James Wilton, was overwhelmed with hate for James and compassion for the gentle, innocent 14 year old girl who had to endure such an indignity. As they walked, he was speechless. He could not find the words he wanted to say to dear Nancy.

She continued her story. "Just as he was about to bring the bailing hook down on me, the barn door sprang open and there was his mother, standing in shock and disgust at what her son had done and was about to do to a 14 year old girl. On her face, you could see the shock and pain, as she gazed upon my nakedness and the rage that was stirring her son to commit murder."

Monte thought back to the times he had looked with disfavour and contempt on Nancy. He found himself near tears, as he reflected on the snide and crude comments he had made about her so many times to so many people. A genuine feeling of shame overwhelmed him. Yes, he thought, you never really know anyone until you have walked in their shores.

Nancy could see the pain the story was causing Monte. Yet, she felt that she must continue. "His mother screamed at him to stop, to not do it. He put the bailing hook by his side, turned to her, almost pleading and said that if he didn't do it, I would tell and she would lose her only child for a long time, maybe forever. She kept pleading with him, but he told her that he had no choice. I knew in my heart that it was all over for me. I knew I could plead and beg for my life but that it would do no good. Everyone knew how much Mrs. Wilton loved that boy, and how in her mentally challenged state that she catered to his every whim. Anyway, when it came to her son, there was no right or wrong – only her son and her love for him. What chance did I have? She would not sacrifice her son for me."

"Again, he raised the bailing hook above his head. Just as he started to bring it down ferociously onto me, his mother reached for a pitch fork that was propped against the stall and as she screamed no, no, she plunged it into his side. The bailing hook fell onto my stomach, slightly cutting me with its sharp edge. James fell to his knees, bleeding profusely as he looked up at his mother in surprise. She dropped to her knees and embraced him, sobbing that she loved him. He gently fell into her arms as she sat there holding him, sobbing uncontrollably. He said not a single word. She begged him to hold on, but as I lay there in disbelief that I was still alive, he died in her arms."

"Mr. Wilton walked into the barn and deduced, without explanation, what had occurred. He grabbed a horse blanket that was hanging above the stall and gently placed it over my naked body. He turned to his wife, knelt down and gently removed his dead son from her hands. Through tears he said that she had to do it - that James was a bad seed and that no matter how much they loved him that was a fact they could not deny. She could have not stood by and watched him continue to brutalize a young girl. He turned to me and ask if I was O.K. Oddly, even though James had cruelly violated me, I felt intensely sorry for the both of them. It was their son who had hurt me, not them. At that moment, I felt more sorry for them than myself."

Monte, mesmerized and shocked by all he had heard found the strength to ask, "but why were the police not notified? Why was he buried out in the honeysuckle grove?"

"Monte, they were going to notify the police, but Mr. Wilton kept saying that now they would take her away from him for sure. She would finally be put in a home for the mentally challenged, where she would die of loneliness and sorrow being separated from him. As we all three walked toward their house, I could not help but feel intense sorrow for what was going to happen to these two people, because they had shielded me from harm. It was then that I suggested to Mr. Wilton that there was no need to call the police. That I was willing to keep what happened a secret for their benefit. In fact, I pleaded with them not to tell anyone, because they should not suffer for the sins of their son. He had gathered up my torn clothing and told me to go into the bedroom and get dressed as quickly as possible, while he and his wife sat and talked about my proposal. I made them promise not to call the police until I returned."

"We discussed it at some length, and I managed to finally, after much persuading, convince Mr. Wilton to bury his son and simply tell everyone that he had disappeared without a word. That night, I helped him wrap his son in three old blankets and we buried him where you saw me and Mrs. Wilton tonight. She goes out there with me every Monday and cries over her beloved son, whom she slay to save me."

"Nancy I am overwhelmed. It is an incredible story."

"Yes, Monte, I feel fortunate to be alive. If not for Mrs. Wilton, I would be the one in the grave. But, that is not all of the story."

Monte in shock replied, "there's more?"

"Yes, we thought all was fine until a few months after the event. I am sure you can guess what I found out at that time."

Monte blurted out, "pregnant."

"Yes, Monte, I was pregnant. Out of concern for what might happen to Mr. and Mrs. Wilton, I could tell no one who the father was, so I just told everyone I did not know, but I did, because I was a virgin when I was raped. It was a violent act, and I abhor how Jasmine was conceived, but it is not her fault, and I must protect her, too."

Monte, almost exhausted from listening to the litany of woe that had been spun by the lovely Nancy said, "I am so sorry Nancy. It must have been a terrible burden on you to carry this for all these years, knowing that you were virtuous when almost everyone but Lenny and Tipper looked on you as a harlot."

"Monte, I learned long ago to not be concerned with what people think of me. I know who and what I am, and I carry no shame. Those who judge me are the ones who carry the shame."

"Nancy, your secret is forever locked in my memory, and I shall never share it with anyone. In fact, the two of us need never speak of it again after this night."

She turned her head toward Monte and smiled. No more talk was necessary. Monte reached down and took her hand. The two of them walked down the dark road, heading toward the lights of the town. Finally, the mystery of Nancy Running Elk was solved.

EPILOGUE
THAT WAS NICE: I HOPE YOU DO IT AGAIN

The rest of the week was spent in intense preparation for the three round robin games that Cree Lake would have to play in Saskatoon in order to reach the Provincial Championship game. Cree Lake played one game on Friday and two games Saturday. Then, the two teams with the most total points would meet Sunday afternoon for the Provincial Championship.

Cree Lake breezed through their first three games without allowing a goal. Sunday, now at 41-0, they were meeting the Moose Jaw team for the championship. As they dressed for the game, Monte kept looking at Nancy and thinking about all she had come to mean to him over the past few months. He was finally realizing that there was more he wanted out of the relationship than just to be friends. That night at the Wilton's made him understand she was not only a person of high character and substance, based upon what she had done to protect the Wilton's from harm, she was the kindest, most compassionate person he had ever known. She had paid a tremendous price for the good she had done. Her moral character had been called into question and nearly the entire town assumed things about her that were grossly inaccurate. Through it all, she continued to hold her head high and effectively carry out her duties as a teenage mother. This was a young woman who struggled valiantly against what many would consider insurmountable odds, and she never once asked for sympathy from the paragons of virtue who pointed fingers of condemnation at her without realizing what she had been through. Now, she sat on the bench, lacing up her skates to go forth and do battle on another field of honour.

164

Coach Wellman watched his team with pride. They were calm and focused, and as they prepared to go out on the ice, he wondered if he could find the words to express what he wanted to say. Never at a loss for words, this night, he felt inadequate to explain to them what this year had meant to him as a coach.

As always, before the start of the game, a hush fell over the locker room as all eyes turned toward the coach. Thus began what would turn out to be Coach Wellman's last pre-game speech.

"Gentlemen," and then he intentionally turned to Myrna and Nancy, who were sitting beside one another, as he said, "and ladies. I am not going to tell you that this is the most important night of your lives, because it isn't. There will be many nights much more important than this one. After all, this is just a game. However, this season and this night will forever live in your hearts. Regardless of the outcome of tonight's game, I want each and everyone of you to know how proud I am to have each one of you call me coach."

"This season has not been just about hockey. It has been about each one of you gaining insights into your own lives and realizing the potential you all have for greatness. Each one of you has empowered yourselves with an understanding that when a group of dedicated people work together, there is nothing that they cannot accomplish. I was told by many people that this team was un-coachable. I refused to believe that, because I saw in each one of you an inner greatness that you did not even realize you had. Where others saw a bunch of rogues, I saw a group of young people looking for a purpose to do their best. Where others saw a lack of discipline, I simply saw a group of people looking for a reason to be disciplined."

The coached walked over to Nancy and Myrna. "I saw two young ladies who were willing to put up with any amount of abuse for the privilege of being a part of this team," and then he made a sweeping motion with his hand all about the room, "and I saw each player on this team refuse to let anyone bully these two team-mates just because of their gender."

Coach Wellman began to pace about the room. "You call me coach, but I have learned as much from you as you have learned from me. So, in a way you have been my coach, just as I have been yours. From Nancy over there, I have learned to value tenacity. This is a girl who will simply not quit. No matter how dire the situation, she has the drive, desire and determination to never give up. From Myrna, I have learned the sheer joy one can get from helping others succeed. She had rather make a great pass, than score a goal. From Benson, Larry and Bobby, I have learned patience. They never panic, and it usually pays off. From Hamm, Hatto and Reed, I have learned the art of the possible. They started out weak and unsure of themselves, but they are now three of the most confident players in this room. From Tom, Hoppy and Tony, I have learned to be anticipative. They have a knack for knowing when, where and how something will happen. From Bobby, Ronnie and Langston, I have learned to be more supportive. When things got bad, they were always there with a pat on the back and an encouraging word. From Ronnie and Jake, I have learned the virtues of hard work. They both know how weak they were at the beginning of the season, and they always stayed after practice to work on their own and were constantly asking me for ways they might improve. Robby and Terry, you taught me the value of levity. No matter how bad the situation, somehow you could make all of us laugh about it."

Coach walked nonchalantly over to Ted. "Ted, you taught me the value of trust, because when I would tell you to do something, you did it without question, because you said that you believed in me. What higher compliment could one person pay another than to simply say you trusted them to do what was right."

Walking over to Monte, coach placed his hand on his shoulder and said, "and you Monte, hey, you are the one who taught me the intrinsic value of not judging an athlete's ability by gender. You are the one who insisted I take a look at Nancy."

As he said "Nancy," coach then smiled broadly and continued. "Of course, we are all aware that you like to look at Nancy, too."

Monte lowered his head as everyone in the room, including Nancy, laughed. In fact, Monte was also smiling, because he no longer felt any shame about his feelings for Nancy.

Finally, Coach Wellman walked over to the towering hulk that was Grif. Looking down at him, coach said, "think I forgot you, Grif?"

Grif shrugged his shoulders and coach said, "and Grif, Grif knows he is not the greatest player to ever lace up skates, but Grif taught me that ability can never replace heart. Grif is the player with the greatest heart I have ever seen."

Walking to the centre of the room, Coach Wellman surveyed his team, looking all about, confidently sighing as he took a deep breath and spoke from the heart.

"There is something very powerful about a conversation between people who can establish a deep, human connection. I hope we have done that this year. I believe in the principles that language and conversation are powerful tools. I am not always good at language, but I hope I have been able to help all of you move forward towards the future you seek, not just in the game we all love but in everything you do. Remember that hockey is a metaphor for life. You have certainly given my life more meaning and purpose. Knowing you has been one of the true highlights of my existence. I am not going to tell you that you will win today. However, regardless of what the scoreboard reads, when you skate off the ice, you are not losers as long as you gave the struggle every thing you had. This year, every second of every practice and every second of every game, you have done that. For that reason, regardless of the outcome of today's game, you are all winners. Remember that you can physically lose a battle or a war, but the strong-willed mind can never be conquered. Let's go play hockey."

With a loud roar, the team got up, walked out of the locker room and skated onto the ice before 6,000 wildly cheering fans, who had come to see the two best midget teams in Saskatchewan do battle. Among those fans was a large contingent from Cree Lake. They had trekked through the wet snow of the beginning, muddy spring thaw to get to chartered buses on the old service road outside town to make the journey to Saskatoon. This was their team. The team that had brought a new sense of pride and dignity to a town and First Nations Reserve nestled in the outback of a desolate and oft forgotten corner of the province and country. This was more than a hockey team to the people of Cree Lake. This was their representation of pride, self-esteem, self-respect and self-efficiency.

As Cree Lake skated to their bench, another mighty roar went up as the much larger contingent of fans from Moose Jaw enthusiastically greeted their team. The team skated on the ice with supreme confidence. Having lost only one game all year, and that to an out-of-province team from Edmonton, they were almost arrogant in their boldness and assuredness, as they all, in an intimidating manner, confidently glided by the Cree Lake bench and glared menacingly at their opponents.

It was obvious to Moose Jaw that beating a team from a small town of 1200 was just a formality. After all, Cree Lake had faced much weaker competition all season long; whereas, Moose Jaw had played some of the best teams in the province.

Even Moose Jaw's pitch black jersey's with a skull and cross-bones scrolled across them proudly displaying their team name, *Pirates*, was intimidating. And their size – oh, they were towering hunks of humanity who appeared unable to find uniforms big enough to fit their muscular frames, as the jerseys and pants appeared to form-fit their bodies that seemed to be bulging from the restraint, waiting to burst out and flex taunt, sinewy muscles.

Their mere skate onto the ice indicated an exceedingly intimidating bunch, and as they were spinning about, displaying a nimbleness that excited apprehensions in many a loyal Cree Lake fan's heart, Coach Wellman's team sat with no trepidation, almost laughing at Moose Jaw's display of programmed intimidation. These Cree Lake young people were immune from overt fear. They respected an opponent, but they refused to bow before intimidation and bullying. Yet, they had never faced such a physically imposing team.

Nancy faced a towering behemoth of muscle when the puck was dropped on the ice and play began. There was a furious scramble, but Monte came out of it first-best, for he bore away the ever elusive rubber disc, and managed to carry it some distance down toward Moose Jaw's goal before losing control. Then, the checking by Moose Jaw became fast and furious. Meanwhile, the agile Cree Lake skaters whirled back and forth across the smooth ice with every imaginable turn and twist. Clever plays were continually occurring on either side, and these were greeted with outbursts of enthusiastic cheering. Although the imposing Moose Jaw team tried valiantly to lay waste to each Cree Lake player with furious checks, most times the nimble Cree Lakers either avoided the checks with deft moves or bounced up like a rubber ball when they were hit.

The Cree Lake supporters shouted themselves fairly hoarse from wild cheering over a brilliant dash on the part of Nancy, whereby she outwitted her opponents with incredible moves and stick handling to gently slide the puck to Monte, who shot it home into the cage for the first goal of the game.

Later on, Moose Jaw evened-up the score. When the first twenty minutes had expired, it was 1-1, and Moose Jaw now seemed to realize that their intimidation tactics had not worked, or had they just been too timid in dealing with these upstarts from a tiny backwater town that didn't belong in the big arena and the big game?

After the intermission they went at it once more. So far, Cree Lake had stood tall against the imposing, hulking Moose Jaw players, but the second period would see Moose Jaw decide that the intimidating play had failed, not out of a lack of fear on the part of Cree Lake, but simply because the rough play had not been intimidating enough. Thus, the second period would be one of the fiercest battles ever witnessed in the Provincial Championships. By the end of that period, Cree Lake had been battered and bruised by the fiercest checking team to ever grace the Saskatoon Arena. Cree Lake's players refused to bow before the intimidation, but how long could they continue against the ceaseless fury that was virtually devastating their ranks? They were exhausted from the battle, their bodies aching for relief from the brutal punishment meted out by a team of behemoth giants who saw the Cree Lake players as sheep, waiting to be led to slaughter. Still tied 1-1, the third period, according to the Moose Jaw coach, would be the period that Cree Lake would collapse from exhaustion. This would be the period that Moose Jaw would finally put away this pesky little team from the backwaters of Saskatchewan.

The puck had hardly been dropped before Cree Lake realized that Moose Jaw was determined to literally destroy them in the third period, if it took every ounce of strenuous ability they possessed. The lack of fear exhibited by Cree Lake rankled the hearts of the Moose Jaw players, and they were grimly resolved to "do or die" as one of them said to Nancy, as she skated to the bench, exhausted from avoiding the heavy hitting being laid out by the team. Her reply was pure Nancy Running Elk, "I'll be sure to come to your funeral."

Hearing that, the Cree Lake bench broke out in laughter. Coach Wellman scanned down the bench to the very end. And there he sat, just as he always did. He figured that he would only be called upon if Cree Lake was well in front, but Coach Wellman was about to surprise him.

He showed the vulnerability of a kind-hearted soul in the body of a giant. His strength was not in his size, but in his heart. Thus, Coach Wellman pointed at Grif and uttered the words, "you're up."

How many times had Grif been on the ice during the season? They could be counted on two hands, but this was his time. Grif wondered why the coach would trust him on the ice with the score knotted 1-1. Yet, he remembered what the coach had said about him in the locker room. The coach believed in him, and at this defining moment, Grif believed in himself as a hockey player. This, yes, this was Grif's time.

Coach said nothing to him. He just smiled as Grif's hulking body leaped over the boards, his towering height and weight making him appear to be a spectre rising from the depths of hell to lay waste to all that stood in his path. The Moose Jaw team, as they lined up for the face-off wondered why this giant had been kept on the bench so long. On the Moose Jaw bench, the players leaned forward in awe of the behemoth that stood before them.

When the puck was dropped, Grif immediately laid out the Moose Jaw centre with a devastating check that sent him flying across the ice. Another Moose Jaw player picked up the lose puck, and again, Grif pummelled him like a hurricane coming ashore at full-force on a tropical island. Just then, as the puck scooted lose from the sprawling player's stick, Grif spotted Nancy open on the right wing. Somehow he managed to extend his stick and gently flutter the puck to a waiting Nancy, who streaked over the blue line with a mighty spurt of energy, slamming the puck brilliantly past the out-stretched goalie into the back of the net.

Loud ramblings of great joy swelled up in the crowd, as Cree Lake surged ahead 2-1. Leaving the same line out, Coach Wellman watched artfully as Moose Jaw lined up for the ensuing face-off. Coach looked at Grif and then pointed to two of the Moose Jaw defensemen with a lingering finger that designated them as Grif's next victims. They backed off slightly, as anticipating a devastating encounter with this maniac of mayhem who had suddenly appeared on the ice. The puck was dropped, and Nancy slid it over to Myrna, just as Grif moved toward the two players who were more concerned about surviving Grif than stopping Nancy. She dodged all interference and when finally too hard pressed, managed to send the rubber disc across to Myrna, who continued the fancy work by slamming it artfully over to Monte; who crashed into the cage area and slammed it home. 3-1 and the players did not slap the back of the goal scorer, they found Grif, whose intimidating tactic had made it all possible.

Things began to look brighter as hockey is a fruitful proving ground for clever tactics, and the wisest general usually manages to carry his team to victory over those who may be much more nimble skaters and even smarter with their sticks, but not so able in the line of strategy. It can be just a simple move that alters the plain and suddenly everything tilts one team's way. Grif was not a great stick handler. He was not an adept passer. He certainly was no prolific goal scorer. He was not a great skater, but he was an inspiration. Sometimes, that is all a team needs – inspiration.

The edge in the game had shifted to Cree Lake, thanks to Coach Wellman trusting Grif to change the tide of battle. Somehow, the infusion of Grif brought that spark the team needed.

Demoralized, Moose Jaw simply began to fall apart. The marvellous agility and strategy of Cree Lake led to one goal after the another, as wild applause rang out from the crowd that was mesmerized by the sudden turn of events.

Grif was out on the ice every other shift. No one would have ever dreamed that a player with meagre hockey abilities could prove himself such a marvellous wizard on steel runners. With the score now 6-1, Grif actually stopped his devastating checking, as the opposing players were fearful of coming anywhere near him. Suddenly he fairly dazzled the opposition and even himself with his new-found speed, his eccentric twisting when hotly pursued, and the clever way in which he kept the puck seemingly glued to his stick.

Thanks to the inspiration provided by Grif "Bad Boy" Joe, the Moose Jaw players were plainly disconcerted and seemed to have entirely lost that aggressive spirit so absolutely necessary to victory. They played almost sullenly, as if realizing that it was all over but the shouting.

As the game drew to a close, Coach Wellman rewarded Grif with one last shift on a line with Nancy and Monte. Streaking into the Moose Jaw end, Nancy had a wide open shot, but as she had done in a previous game, she eschewed a guaranteed goal and dropped the puck behind her for Grif to pick up and slam home. True to his nature, Grif, too, decided he did not need a goal to make his day complete, so he slid it over to Monte who drove it home. 7-1 with thirty-three seconds left, and Coach Wellman brought Grif off the ice to the thunderous cheers of the fans who had witnessed an incredible display of sportsmanship and unselfishness from a team that had defied all the odds to win the Provincial Championship.

As the Cree Lake players jubilantly celebrated when the final buzzer sounded, Nancy and Monte removed their helmets, skated up to one another and joyously embraced. Among all the jubilation and excitement, they just stood there staring at one another. Nancy was a miracle of beauty, and she exuded a bold continence as a perky glow seemed to radiate all about her while the arena lights made her long, coal-black hair shine and shimmer. Her dark brown eyes twinkled and her lips puckered as if waiting for a kiss. Then the silence was broken as she said to Monte, "you have been wanting to kiss me since I stole your skates. Are you going to do it or not?

Monte bent forward and again took her in her arms, passionately kissing her as the crowd and both teams cheered their approval. When their lips parted, Nancy said, "that was nice. I hope you do it again."

THE END OR IS IT THE BEGINNING?

VOCABULARY

What follows is intended for the many teachers who use this book in their classes. By no means is this a complete vocabulary list. This is simply a compilation of a few of the words with which some students (depending on individual reading level) in middle school, junior high school or high school might not be familiar. The definitions relate specifically to the way the word is used in this book. (USA spelling is listed second.)

From The Prologue

metaphor: A figure of speech in which a word or phrase that ordinarily designates one thing is used to designate another, thus making an implicit comparison, as in *"a sea of troubles"* or *"All the world's a stage"* (Shakespeare).

dementia: Deterioration of intellectual faculties, such as memory, concentration, and judgment, resulting from an organic disease or a disorder of the brain. It is sometimes accompanied by emotional disturbance and personality changes. Madness or insanity.

inextricable: So intricate or entangled as to make escape impossible: an inextricable maze; an inextricable web of deceit. Difficult or impossible to disentangle or untie: an inextricable tangle of threads. Too involved or complicated to solve: an inextricable problem. Unavoidable; inescapable.

prima-donnas: Temperamental, conceited people.

theocracy: (Government, Business, Politics & Diplomacy) Run by a deity, by a priesthood or a designated supreme authority or authorities.

vanquished: To defeat or conquer in battle; subjugate. To defeat in a contest, conflict, or competition.
To overcome or subdue (an emotion, for example); suppress.

binary: Characterized by or consisting of two parts or components; twofold.

perpetuated: To cause to continue indefinitely; make perpetual. To prolong the existence of; cause to be remembered.

unencumbered: Not burdened with cares or responsibilities.

conventionalities: The state, quality, or character of being conventional. Conventional acts, ideas or practices - the normal way.

From Chapter 1

precariously: Dangerously lacking in security or stability. Subject to chance or unknown conditions.
provocation: The act of provoking or inciting. Something that provokes.
harlot: A prostitute or promiscuous woman
pariah: A social outcast. Untouchable.
piqued: To provoke; arouse.
wistfully: Full of wishful yearning. Pensively sad; melancholy.
bequeath: To leave or give (personal property) by will. To pass (something) on to another; hand down.

From Chapter 2

indignant: Angered at something unjust or wrong
malcontents: A chronically dissatisfied person. One who rebels against the established system.
irreverent: Lacking or exhibiting a lack of reverence; disrespectful. Critical of what is generally accepted or respected; satirical.
consternation: A feeling of anxiety, dismay, dread, or confusion.
paraphernalia: The articles used in a particular activity; equipment.
fathom: To penetrate to the meaning or nature of; comprehend.
ingratiating: Pleasing; agreeable. Calculated to please or win favour
demeanour/demeanor: The way in which a person behaves; deportment.
enamoured/enamored: To inspire with love; captivated.
demure: Affectedly shy, modest, or reserved in behaviour.
manifesting: To be evidence of; prove.
perturbed: To disturb greatly; make uneasy or anxious. To throw into great confusion.

From Chapter 3

tenacity: Persistent determination.
innate: Possessed as an essential characteristic; inherent.
writhed: To twist, as in pain, struggle, or embarrassment.
miscreant: Wrongdoer or villain.
stealthily: Marked by or acting with quiet, caution, and secrecy intended to avoid notice.

From Chapter 4

conspicuously: Easy to notice; obvious. Attracting attention, as by being unusual or remarkable; noticeable.
mundane: Commonplaces; ordinary.
camaraderie: A spirit of familiarity and trust existing between friends.
dossiers: A collection of papers giving detailed information about a particular person or subject.
malcontents: A chronically dissatisfied person. One who rebels against the established system
coalesce: To grow together; fuse. To come together so as to form one whole; unite.
animosity: Bitter hostility, open enmity; active hatred.
admonition: Cautionary advice or warning.
ecstatic: Great rapture or delight. Showing or feeling great enthusiasm.
adroitly: Skilful (skillful-USA) and adept.
pandemonium: Wild uproar, confusion or noise.

From Chapter 5

nefarious: Evil; wicked; sinful.
protestations: A strong or formal expression of dissent.
contingent: An event or condition that is likely but not inevitable.

From Chapter 6

exuded: To exhibit in abundance. To come forth with.

From Chapter 7

broach: To bring up (a subject) for discussion or debate.
malevolent: Having or exhibiting ill will; wishing harm to others; malicious. Having an evil or harmful influence.
dire: Warning of or having dreadful or terrible consequences; calamitous. Urgent; desperate.
philanthropically: To provide humanitarian or charitable assistance.
felonious: Relating to or concerning a felony (serious crime). Evil; wicked.

cache: A store of goods or valuables concealed in a hiding place.
impudently: Offensive boldness; insolent or impertinent.
homily: An inspirational saying or platitude.
exonerate: To clear or absolve from blame. To relieve from an obligation or task; exempt.
innuendo: : An indirect or subtle implication or insinuation.

Chapter 8

behest: An authoritative order or earnest request.
lugubrious: Excessively mournful, dismal, or gloomy.
sardonic: Scornfully or cynically mocking.
self-deprecating: Tending to undervalue oneself and one's abilities.
sauntering: A leisurely pace, walk or stroll.
adieu: Goodbye; farewell.
forlornly: Appearing sad, lonely, desperate or pitiful.
euphoric: A feeling of great happiness or well-being.

Chapter 9

stoically: Seemingly indifferent to or unaffected by pleasure or pain; impassive.
cower: To cringe in fear.
facade: An artificial or deceptive front.
banal: Drearily commonplace and often predictable; trite.
penchant: A definite liking; a strong inclination.
pensive: Deeply, often wistfully or dreamily thoughtful. Suggestive or expressive of melancholy thoughtfulness.

Chapter 10

sedate: Calm. Keeping a quiet steady attitude or pace.

Chapter 11

paramour: A lover.
surreal: Having an oddly dreamlike quality.
trepidation: A state of alarm or dread; apprehension.
impervious: Not able to be influenced or affected; not receptive.
nonchalantly: Seeming to be coolly unconcerned or indifferent.

translucent: Transmitting light but causing sufficient diffusion to prevent perception of distinct image.
disconcerting: Frustrating, disorder; disarrange.
unabated: Without losing any force or violence; undiminished.
satiated: To satisfy (an appetite or desire) fully.

Chapter 12

apropos: At an appropriate time; opportunely.
irrefutable: Impossible to deny or disprove; incontrovertible.
soliloquy: The act or custom of talking to self and revealing thoughts.
disingenuous: Not sincere; lacking candour.
propitious: Favourable; auguring well. Gracious or favourably inclined.
sanctity: Regarded as sanctified or holy.
innuendo: an indirect or subtle reference, usually made maliciously indicating criticism or disapproval; insinuation.
precipice: The brink of a dangerous or disastrous situation.
propensity: A natural tendency or disposition.
litany: Any long or tedious speech or recital. Can sometimes refer to a long list.
cognizant: Fully informed; conscious; aware of.
probity: Complete and confirmed integrity; uprightness.
corroborate: To confirm or support the facts, opinions, etc.
castigation: Criticizing severely.
impugn: To challenge or attack as false; assail; criticize.
decorum: Appropriateness of behaviour or conduct; propriety.
credence: Acceptance as true or valid.
cunningly: Artful subtlety and deceptiveness.
unmitigated: Without qualification or exception; absolute.
emanating: To send forth; emit.
bombastic: Lofty acting; pompous.
indomitable: Difficult or impossible to defeat or subdue.
promulgated: To make known.

Chapter 13

cavalierly: Offhand disregard; dismissive.
sequestered: Remove or set apart; segregate.
clandestinely: Kept or done in secret, often in order to conceal an

illicit or improper purpose.
morph: To be transformed.
mystique: An aura of heightened value or interest or meaning surrounding a person or thing.
enigma: A person, thing, or situation that is mysterious, puzzling, or ambiguous,
inconspicuous: Not easily noticed or seen; not prominent or striking.
cornucopia: Abundant supply or source.

Chapter 14

mesmerized: To spellbind; enthral (enthrall – USA).

Epilogue

intrinsic: Of or relating to the essential nature of a thing; inherent.
sinewy: Lean and muscular. Strong and vigorous.
behemoth: Something enormous in size or power.
deft: Quick and skilful (skillful-USA)
eschewed: To keep clear of or abstain from; shun; avoid

Definitions from Farlex International Dictionary

If YOU ENJOYED THIS BOOK ABOUT HOCKEY – READ
***HOW HOCKEY SAVED A JEW FROM THE HOLOCAUST:
THE RUDI BALL STORY***
Available from your local bookstore or Amazon.com